D1055380

THE ANNOYANCE BUREAU

THE BIG THINGS WE LEAVE TO FATE.
THE REST BELONGS TO

LUCY FRANK

A RICHARD JACKSON BOOK
ATHENEUM BOOKS FOR YOUNG READERS
NEW YORK LONDON TORONTO SYDNEY SINGAPORE

Atheneum Books for Young Readers
An imprint of Simon & Schuster Children's Publishing Division
1230 Avenue of the Americas
New York, New York 10020
Book design by O'Lanso Gabbidon
The text for this book is set in New Caledonia.
Printed in the United States of America
First Edition
10 9 8 7 6 5 4 3 2 1
Library of Congress Cataloging-in-Publication Data
Frank, Lucy.
The annoyance bureau / Lucy Frank.
p.   cm.
"A Richard Jackson book."
Summary: While spending his Christmas vacation in New York
City with his father and new stepfamily, twelve-year-old Lucas meets
a rebellious agent of the secret Annoyance Bureau, which exists to
control or eliminate all sources of annoyance in the modern world.
ISBN 0-689-84903-6
[1. Stepfamilies—Fiction. 2. Christmas—Fiction. 3. New York (N.Y.)—
Fiction. 4. Humorous Stories.] I. Title.
PZ7.F8515 An 2002
[Fic]—dc21   2001053732

For Dick

And in memory of my brother, Paul, who could have
used a little magic

CHAPTER 1

"Thank you for doing this for me," Mom said as we sat in the car outside Dad's building. "Thanks for letting me take this vacation. Just remember, Lucas. They love you."

"Right," I said. "They love me."

As in, "I love Lucas dearly. I just wish he were a little more, how shall I put this . . . a little less . . ." Which I'd overheard Dad's wife say last time I came to New York City, Columbus Day weekend.

Mom knew what I'd been thinking. I could tell. "Okay," she said. "One more time. Survival tip number one?"

"Don't take it personally," I said.

"And survival tip number two?"

"Don't take it personally."

"Exactly." She nodded. We'd spent the drive down making lists of ways to get me through this week. We'd packed up the Christmas gifts Mom had bought me, dropped my dog, Aslan, at the kennel, and headed here as soon as I got home from school. "And number three?"

I knew I was supposed to say "DTIP" again. "Bring a lot of books."

She laughed. I'd just added that one. "Don't read them at the table, though," she warned. "Or walking down the street."

"Or in the bathroom. Ever," I said. "On pain of death." In Dad's apartment I had to share a bathroom with my stepsister, Phoebe.

Mom's face went serious again. "Listen. Try to remember, okay? Number one, none of this is easy for Phoebe, either. Two, you're all still in the adjustment stage. Three, with a new baby in the family . . . Four, your dad and Claire are both working very long hours, so if they seem tense . . ."

We were drawing out this list making, both of us. After a certain point it was easier just to leave.

She hugged me.

"Oh, dear," she said, trying to get the clump of my hair that never stayed down to stay down. "Now I'm wishing I'd insisted on that haircut."

I didn't realize till the car had pulled away that I hadn't told her to have a great week in the Bahamas.

Dad's eyes went straight to my hair as soon as he opened the apartment door. "Welcome, welcome! Come on in. We've been waiting for you." I could see him trying to decide if he should shake my hand or hug me. He shook my hand. Then he gave me a sort of thump on the shoulder. *This boy goes to Bentley Prep*, I could see him thinking. *Why does he still look like this?*

"Keep your coat on," Claire said after she'd kissed me. She looked like she was trying to resist the urge to reach over and pat down my hair too. "You can leave those bags here. We're going right out. We waited to choose a Christmas tree till you arrived, right, Calvin?"

Calvin had his snowsuit on and was sitting in his stroller. "Woof!" he said, bouncing up and down. "Woof, woof! Woof!"

I'd taught him to bark on Columbus Day. That was a long time ago for someone who wasn't even two. Calvin was cool.

"Grrrrr, Calvin!" I growled back at him.

"Grrrr!" He grinned at me.

"No growling, sweetie," Claire told him. "Say 'Hello, Lucas.' Lucas, you know I'd really appreciate if you wouldn't encourage him."

"Sorry," I said.

"The other children in his play group are saying 'Mama' and 'Dada,'" she said. "Some of the little girls are speaking in whole sentences. It's embarrassing to have a child who only barks."

"Sorry," I said again.

"Not a problem," Dad said. "Phoebe," he called. "Lucas is here. We're leaving."

Phoebe came in carrying her cell phone and pulling on her black leather jacket, followed by Tinkerbell the cat. She looked me up and down. So did Tinkerbell. *Oh, yes. We remember you,* I could see him thinking. *But do we hate you? Hmm. We might. Let's see.* He sniffed my legs.

"He smells Aslan," I told Dad.

Phoebe raised her eyebrow. "He smells *something,*" she said too softly for Dad or Claire to hear.

Don't take it personally, I told myself as we rode down in the elevator. I'd dropped my duffel and the shopping bag, but I still had my backpack on. It was stupid, I knew, carrying fifty pounds of sci-fi books to get a Christmas tree. But for some reason I felt better having my stuff with me. More like me. Safer.

"So, how's school going? How is the old place?" Dad asked. Dad had gone to Bentley too.

"Fine," I said.

"Your mom tells me you're keeping your grades up."

"Pretty much," I said. I wished I'd stopped in the bath-room before we left. I wished everyone wasn't looking at me.

"So, you going out for any sports?"

He already knew the answer to that. "Not really."

Maybe it would be better once we got outside and over to Broadway and they forgot about me and focused on finding a tree.

Broadway was full of Christmas tree vendors. "Yeah, that one's okay," I said each time Dad or Claire asked me for a tree opinion. "Yeah, that's a nice one."

"Oh. You're saying you like lopsided trees with no branches," Phoebe said when I said I liked one of Claire's choices.

"No. I think not." Claire nixed Phoebe's choice. "It's a little small. And not full enough. I was hoping for a really full one."

"You've got to be kidding," Dad said about mine. "I'll get a plastic tree before I pay a hundred twenty dollars. Excuse me. Sir, can we see one a bit smaller?"

By the time we'd gotten to our fourth tree seller, I'd come up with a new Lucas survival tip: Stay out of it. That probably wouldn't work either.

I could see Calvin wasn't enjoying this any more than I was. "Calvin. What do cats say?" I said, since Claire had asked me not to bark.

Calvin perked up. "Woof."

"That's dogs, Calvin," I said. "What does Tinkerbell say?"

"Roof!" he said. For a baby his voice was really low. Loud, too. I had to laugh.

Claire threw me a look. "Now, don't get me wrong, Charles," I heard her tell Dad. "I'm one of Lucas's biggest fans. . . ."

"Lucas!" Dad said.

"Sorry," I said.

There was a giant inflatable Frosty the Snowman on the awning of a fruit market. The wind made him look like he was doing the Macarena. I watched him for a while. I watched people try to tiptoe through the slush without messing up their shoes. I watched a scruffy guy with long, stringy hair get people to give him money so he'd stop singing. "Rrrrrrollin'"—he was carrying a boom box and singing into a mike, so I could hear him clearly—"rrrrrrollin'!" His voice was horrible. "Rrrrrrrrollin' on the river!"

It was interesting how many people fit on these sidewalks. It was amazing how stressed they all seemed. One lady had hung so many shopping bags on her stroller that when she let go of the handles for a second, it tipped over backward. Then she screamed at her kid. I watched a businessman-type guy kick a taxicab and yell, "What, you're gonna hit me?" as he crossed the street against the light. Even the dogs here looked stressed. I'd been wishing Aslan could have come with me. Maybe he was lucky he was in the kennel.

I noticed some guys with walkie-talkies going by, saying things like "Roger that," and "Over and out," and "Copy," hurrying down the street like, *Do not mess with me. I am highly official and extremely important.* "Possible rumpus at Computer Town," I thought I heard one say. "No. Change that to confirmed ruckus. Potential fisticuffs at Foodway." That couldn't be what they were saying. They *were* dressed somewhat strangely, though—long, rumply green coats, and hats like men wear in old movies. I'd seen eight of them by now. No, nine. And this one was a woman. "Gridlock at Toy Fair cash registers," she was saying. "Do you read me?" Maybe they were making a movie. I'd seen that other times

5

I'd been here. There were no cameras, though. And nobody on the street seemed to be paying attention.

"Rrrrrrollin'. Rrrrrrrollin' . . ." Scruffy was headed our way. I was interested to see what Dad and Claire and Phoebe would have to say to him. He had his hand out. "Spare some change? A penny, a quarter, a dollar? Rrrrrrrrollin' on the—"

"Noise pollution near Book World," a walkie-talkie guy said as he hurried by me. "Request removal authorization. Over."

The mike Scruffy had been holding vanished. His mouth was still moving, but there was no sound coming out. He just stood there staring at his empty hand.

"First removal achieved. Proceeding to hot spot at Book World," I heard the walkie-talkie guy say.

Book World was just down the block. I could see two more men with hats and green coats out front helping some Salvation Army guys set up their kettle and their amplifier.

Dad and Claire were deep in discussion about a tree. Phoebe was talking on her phone. Calvin had conked out. I started toward Book World.

As I got close a man in a Santa Claus suit ran out the bookstore door. "What'd you just do?" he shouted at the walkie-talkie guys.

I moved closer.

"Routine abatement," said the one who'd requested the removal. "Unauthorized noise pollution of a nonholiday nature."

"Oh, and you think this is better?" Santa pointed toward the Salvation Army guys, who'd started playing "Silent Night" on bugle and tambourine. The bugle player was not good.

"HQ orders," one of the other walkie-talkie guys

answered. He was tall and lumpy. His partner was short and weaselly. "They were in front of Macy's. HQ said move 'em, and we moved 'em."

"Well, move them somewhere else," Santa said. "This is my territory. Book World and all annoyances appurtenant thereto."

I walked closer.

"And that abatement of yours abated my Muzak," Santa said.

"It's gone?" The removal guy looked puzzled. "Totally gone?"

"'Totally gone?'" Santa mocked. "Yes, Elpidio. What a shock. Your so-called routine abatement abated something that was helping. Per usual."

Something in Santa's hand was beeping loudly. I checked to make sure Dad was still busy. Then I went over to the store window and tried to look like I was book shopping.

Santa had stopped the beeping. "That Muzak in the store was reducing levels. Unlike this preposterous blatting." He nodded toward the bugle player. "And why is this new slush here suddenly? Does Book World need Park Avenue's slush? I don't think so."

All of Broadway was pretty soupy. There was yucky gray snow piled up at every curb. But now that I looked, there did seem to be about six times as much around Book World.

Santa glanced at me. "I'm glad somebody here agrees with me."

I'd been trying not to stare. He'd caught me.

"You know," he told the walkie-talkie guys, "if I were a different kind of guy, I'd be taking this personally."

Taking this personally? This was either a very big coincidence or very weird.

"Don't get your shorts in a knot," he called to me. "Stick

around. It's just getting interesting." He nodded toward a very large woman walking up to them. She had on the same green coat and a big fur hat. "Hey there, toots," he called to her.

"What's the problem?" she asked the walkie-talkie guys. "Is our associate here having a snit?" With the hat, she seemed a foot taller than Santa. She shook her finger at him. "No snits. Remember? The guidelines forbid snits."

Santa glanced at me again, then drew himself up taller. "My dear Hildegund," he said, "there are five days till Christmas, the five most difficult days of the year. If you would forget the guidelines for a second, you might actually get something done. You might even, heavens to Murgatroyd, reduce annoyance levels, which in the last two minutes have gone from ridiculously irritating to abominably vexatious."

I changed my mind. There was no way I was leaving.

"Look around you," he said. "He's irked. She's irked. Anyone with the brains of an anchovy is irked. And what are you doing about it? That's what I'd like to know. Because I know what I'm doing!" I'd assumed the beeping thing was a cell phone, but when he held it out, I could see it was too big. "Watch this," he told me.

"You're not allowed to have that!" the removal guy warned.

"Give me the device," the short guy said. "Come on, now"—he stepped closer—"hand it over."

"Back off, Casimir!" Santa warned.

"It's not approved. It has not been authorized. The regs strictly prohibit—"

"I wouldn't worry about it," the woman said. "It doesn't work."

"Doesn't work?" Santa said. "Doesn't work? This baby

works beyond your wildest dreams. This baby can change the face of . . ."

He held it out and pressed some buttons.

Beedle-dee-BEEP-bee-beeeeep! It went off. The woman grabbed for it.

Beep-BEE-bee-dee-BEE-bee-dee-BEEEE! Santa scooted away.

"Come on, now, old buddy," the tall guy said. "Calm down. Chill. Relax. Give us the thing!"

"Thing?" Santa hid his hands behind his back. "What *thing?* The only things I'm seeing are a bunch of burned-out bureaucrats who wouldn't know an annoyance from an armadillo, a nuisance from a knockwurst, a pest from a prune danish. . . ." He lowered his voice. "Pssst!" He signaled with his head for me to come over. I edged closer. "Help me out, here," he whispered.

"Son!" Uh-oh. Dad was calling me. "What are you doing over there?"

I turned around. Dad had a humongous tree on his shoulder. Phoebe looked disgusted. Calvin was crying. "I know, sweetie," Claire was telling him. "I should have brought your Cheerios. But we're going to get a nice pizza. No. Leave your mittens on, Calvin. Don't take your mittens off."

"Requesting backup!" I heard the woman say. "Meltdown at Book World. Yes, of course it's him. Who else?"

"Erupt, maybe," Santa shouted over her. "Melt, not likely!" I felt a tug on my backpack. "Don't let this out of your sight," he whispered. "Don't let anyone see it. And do not, whatever you do, push any buttons. Lucas"—I felt him unzip the outside pocket and slip something in—"I know I can count on you."

He knew my name?

"Uh . . . you know . . . I don't really think—" I started to say.

"Lucas," Dad called. "I could use a hand here. This tree is not light."

"Let's figure out what we're going to order, okay?" Claire said. "Lucas, what do you like on your pizza?"

"Can we not get whole wheat this time, please?" Phoebe said. "I hate the whole wheat. It's like eating cardboard."

"Lucas, what are you doing?" Dad asked.

What I was doing was taking my pack off so I could give Santa back whatever this thing was. But by the time I'd turned, Santa and the walkie-talkie guys were gone.

CHAPTER 2

I went straight to my room when we got home, closed the hall door and the bathroom door, and opened the pack. I'd worried the whole way that Santa's gizmo might explode inside it, or that one of the walkie-talkie guys would snatch it off my back, but the device was still there. It wasn't ticking or flashing. I took it out.

It didn't look like a bomb. It looked like an oversize remote, but with a screen like a cell phone, two knobs on each end, and a ton of buttons. It didn't seem to open. It had no antenna, no place for batteries, no numbers, no words, no arrows. Nothing that said what it was or how to turn it on. Not that I planned to try.

Claire knocked on the door. "Lucas, aren't you joining us?"

"In a second." The doors to this room didn't lock. They didn't latch right either. Tinkerbell bashed his way in on a regular basis, and last time I was down, I was sure someone went through my things. Whatever this gizmo was, I couldn't leave it here. I unpacked, arranged my books, stuck the thing in my pocket, and went out to the living room.

Dad was setting up the Christmas tree. "Yes, Claire. I

know it's crooked. That's why I'm adjusting it." He tightened the screw on one side of the stand.

"A smidge to the left," Claire said. "No, too much! Charles, I said a smidge."

"Want me to help, Dad?" I said.

"No, thanks. I'm fine—"

"Not that way, Dad!" Phoebe said. "Dad, you're making it worse!"

Dad? Last time I was here, she had called him Charles, like Claire did. Which also sounded weird to me. Mom called him Charlie.

I checked my watch. Mom's plane had just left.

"Why don't you relax, Lucas." Claire smiled at me. "Make yourself at home."

It wasn't relaxing having this gizmo in my pocket. Plus, I was never sure if Claire meant go away and relax, or stay and relax. She kept an eye on her white furniture whenever I was in here.

Tinkerbell sauntered over to see if he'd changed his mind about me. I held my hand out for him to sniff. His ears went back. He hissed. He meowed. "Meow" turned to "Rrrrowww." The "Rrrrowww" turned to retching. "Tink, not on the carpet! Why is it always on my white carpet?" Claire grabbed him around the stomach and carried him to the front hall, where the floor was tiled. She put him down just in time.

"Wow. He really likes you, Lucas," Phoebe whispered to me. Then she left.

I went over and examined the tubular black blob of throw-up. Calvin came with me. "Uh, is that a mouse?" I said. It looked like a mouse. Aslan caught mice all the time.

"Calvin, honey, don't touch it!" Claire lifted him away. "It's a hair ball, Lucas."

"I always thought hair balls were round," I said. "Or maybe that's only if you have a round cat."

Aslan could swallow Tinkerbell in one bite. That would be a hair ball.

"You know, Claire"—Dad picked up the hair ball with a tissue—"as long as you've got Calvin captured, we should give him his bath."

"Woof!" Calvin said.

Claire frowned at me. "Let me catch Phoebe before she gets on the phone," she said. "You two can decorate the tree."

"You'd better let me do all the valuable glass ones and the antiques," Phoebe told me the second we were alone. She was on her phone.

Bzzzzzzzt! The gizmo went off in my pocket. I felt it more than heard it, a buzzy vibration like an electric toothbrush or something.

"Are you listening, Lucas? You can do the, like, pinecones and the cheesy ones."

"Fine." The buzzing had stopped. I picked up a striped metal ball with a spike thing on the end and hung it on a branch.

"Hold on, Zo," she said into the phone. "That doesn't go there," she told me. "It goes on the top." I put it on the top. "Who do you think?" she told the phone person. "My, quote, stepbrother." She started giggling. "Yes! No!" She glanced over at me. "Zoë wants to know if you're a hottie. Uh, Zo"—she cracked up—"I thought we'd had that discussion. Yes. He's standing right here. Lucas, not the side of the top. The tippy top."

Bzzzzt! There it was again. It'd be funny if it turned out to be an alarm clock. Or a garage door opener with no door to open.

"Okay." I reached as high as I could and hooked the little hook over a branch. The ball fell off onto the carpet.

"Lucas!" Phoebe did this giant slump-sigh. "Trust me, Zoë," she said into the phone. "He's not your type. Why? Because he looks like a Chia Pet. No. Not the bod. The hair."

BZZZZZZZZT! Or maybe it was some weird kind of beeper. Maybe Santa was beeping me. Trying to send me a message. I needed to look at it again.

"Where are you going, Lucas?" Phoebe said when I started to leave. "You're supposed to be helping." She studied my hair again. "Uh, like an animal sat down on his head? And then died? I don't know." She giggled. "A hedgehog? A woodchuck? No, it's a badger. A large, dead badger who needs a bath. Or maybe that's how they're wearing it at the Berkley School."

I considered reminding her that it was Bentley Prep, not Berkley. I considered telling her that badgers were striped. I considered stabbing her with the spiked ball. *Don't take it personally,* I told myself. Then I picked up a pinecone elf guy by his stocking cap and chucked it at her head. I missed. The cap came off in my hand.

"No!" she was telling Zoë. "You wouldn't like him. I know so. A, he's twelve—"

"For one more month," I said.

She ignored me. "B"—she picked up a glass icicle and hung it on the tree—"he's extremely immature. And just in case a C is needed, he has zero social skills."

I was thinking more about my throwing skills.

"Uh, Lucas"—she raised her eyebrow—"are you just putting things anyplace you feel like? Because that's not the way we do it. We have systems around here—"

"Woof!" Calvin ran in, sopping wet and, except for the

pajama pants on his head, naked. "Woof! Woof, woof! Grrrrrrrrr!"

"Not funny, Calvin. Calvin. Stop. Calvin. Come back here!" Dad ran in with a towel and scooped him up.

Then Claire came in wiping bubble bath off her arm. "So. How're you guys doing?" She smiled at me.

"We're doing just fine." Phoebe gave her a big, phony smirk.

"Fine," I said.

"You know, Lucas, honey," Claire said. "We've been meaning to talk to you. Your dad and I are very glad you're here, but . . ."

Here we go, I thought. *Here it comes.*

"We're a little concerned about what you're going to do for eight days. We're so swamped at work, and with Christmas coming up and all . . ."

They were both lawyers, at the same firm. Lawyers worked all the time. It was one of the reasons I didn't come down often. Also why Dad didn't drive up to take me out that much anymore.

"We need to go into the office tomorrow, in fact," Dad said. "We're lucky we're getting to take off Christmas Eve day and Christmas. Come on, Calvin. Let's get a diaper on you, buddy. Great job with the tree, Lucas. Will you excuse us?"

"Sure," I said. "It's fine."

But Claire went on apologizing, explaining about big clients, important meetings, seeing her trainer, getting her legs waxed, Christmas shopping.

I kept telling her it was fine, but I wasn't really listening. I was thinking it was fine they'd be at work too. I'd go to my room, close the doors, and read. For the next eight days.

"Of course, Gladys will be in every day," Claire said. "It's a good thing she lives in the building. I don't know what we'd do without Gladys. She's practically one of the family."

Now I was listening. I'd met Gladys. Gladys was the baby-sitter. Gladys was scary.

"She'll make you breakfast tomorrow, and then you can go with them to Toddler Gym. And there's this fabulous new indoor playground. I hope you're not too bored. Phoebe's going out shopping with her friends, but they'll come back here after. Which might be fun for you."

Phoebe did her slump-sigh, made sure Claire wasn't looking, and stuck her finger down her throat.

Bzzzzzzzzzzzzzzzt! It seemed like the gizmo wanted to get away from her as much as I did.

"Would you excuse me?" I said. "I think I'm going to go to bed."

I said good night to Dad and Calvin and went into the bathroom between my room and Phoebe's. Tinkerbell was standing on the sink licking my toothbrush.

"No, Tinkerbell!" I said. "Tink, stop that!"

Tink looked up at me like, *Is there a problem?* and kept licking.

"Yes. There is. You just threw up. Tinkerbell"—I tried to make my voice kind but firm—"get down!"

Make me, his eyes said.

I pushed him down.

It was Tink's tail that knocked down all of Phoebe's beauty products. But his eyes said, *Uh-oh. You're in trouble now, Lucas.*

There were at least thirty jars and bottles on the floor. How had they been arranged? Light to dark? Dark to light? By brand? All the body washes together, or green-apple lip-gloss next to green-apple body wash next to green nail polish? Phoebe had a system for everything. Her systems never made sense. I dumped everything back onto the counter, doused my toothbrush in Listerine to kill the cat cooties, went into my room, took off my clothes, put the gizmo in the nightstand drawer, got into bed, and tried to read.

Scritch, scritch. "Meow!"

Oh, no. Tinkerbell was still in the bathroom.

I ignored him. He'd bashed his way in here a hundred times before.

He meowed louder.

"Lucas!" Phoebe yelled from her room. "Let him in!"

A buzz came from the drawer. Maybe Santa was trying to get me to answer him. I reached over and pulled out the gizmo. It didn't look like any device I'd ever seen. It was about six inches long. Three wide. One inch thick. And it had forty-eight buttons.

Tink was still meowing.

"Lucas! He wants you to let him in."

He was her cat. Why didn't she let him into her room?

He meowed louder.

I opened the bathroom door, sure he'd run right to the other door and meow to be let out. Instead he jumped on my bed, sat on my pillow, and began to lick himself.

Forty-eight buttons. Why would anyone need forty-eight buttons? And what was that strange doohickey sticking out the top, not to mention the two knobs on each side? It'd be great if one of them adjusted the brightness. Then I could see the display, see if there was a phone number on it, or even a message. Santa'd told me not to touch the buttons. He'd said nothing about the knobs. I gave the bigger one a turn. It fell off. I put it on again and tried the other one.

The screen got no brighter, but Tinkerbell leaped up and began to chase his tail. I gave the knob another turn. He whirled faster. This had to be a coincidence. I turned the knob a little more. Round and round he ran, in tighter and tighter circles. I never knew cats could spin so fast. His tongue was hanging out. He looked totally crazed. I had to laugh. I was a little worried, though. He'd already thrown up once today. I turned the knob all the way back. He stopped whirling, flopped onto the pillow, and, giving me a look like *Whooh! That was excellent!*, passed out. I could have sworn he was smiling.

I moved him to the rug so I could lie down. He didn't even open his eyes.

Very weird. Too weird. This gizmo was going back in the drawer.

A cry came from the bathroom. "I don't believe this, Chloe! I had all my cosmetics carefully arranged, and there's, like, Listerine and dandruff in the sink, and he left the toilet seat up! Do you think I should say something to him?"

I jumped into bed.

"I'm *going* to say something to him. I don't care if he's sleeping. Lucas?" She knocked. "Are you awake in there? Oh, I don't believe this. He got Crest on my towel. Lucas!"

The door opened. I pretended to be asleep.

BZZZZZZZZZZZZT! The gizmo went off inside the drawer. Maybe if I started snoring, she wouldn't notice it.

"Lucas! What did you do?" she screamed. "You killed my cat! Chloe, I'll call you back!"

Bzzzzzzzzzt! Bzzz-bzzzzt! BZZZZZZZT! The thing was rattling and vibrating against the wood.

I snored louder.

"Tink? Tinkerbell?" I heard Phoebe say. "Tinkie boy? Are you okay? Lucas. What did you do to him? Why is he just lying there? Why is he smiling like that?"

Snoring had not been a good idea. Now I had to keep snoring till she left.

"He looks drunk! Lucas, did you give him Listerine?"

If I opened my eyes and told her that was the stupidest thing I'd ever heard, she'd get even madder.

"Lucas. Stop snoring. That is so not amusing. I know you're not sleeping. All the lights are on. Lucas, are you doing this purposely to annoy me?"

Me annoy her? I was the one lying here trying to mind my own business. Instead of a remote-control cat-whirler beeper gizmo, Santa should have given me one of those walkie-talkies. "Annoyance emergency at the Grahams'. Do you read me?" That's what I'd be saying now. "Request removal authorization. Get me out of here. Over."

CHAPTER
3

The one thing more annoying than Phoebe was Gladys.

"Good morning, Lukey Sunshine! Wakey, wakey!"

I'd barely recovered from last night. I pulled the blanket over my head.

"Are you sleep-ing, are you sleep-ing? Bro-ther Luke, Bro-ther Luke?"

Please don't sing, Gladys.

Bzzzzt! The gizmo went off inside the drawer.

"Knock, knock! Rise and shine! I have a little furry friend here who's waiting to say hello! Yoo-hoo! Are you alive in there?"

Bzzzzzt! Bzzzzt! I reached an arm out, brought the gizmo under the covers with me, then burrowed in deeper.

She opened the door. "Hel-lo, Lukey Dukey!"

Was this supposed to be her Tinkerbell voice?

She was coming closer. *Do not tickle me, Gladys. You tickle me, you die.*

Whomp. She dumped Tink onto my back. "Come out and play, Lucas!"

Bzzzzzzzzzzzzzzzzzzzzzzzzzzzzzzzzzt! This sounded urgent. I had no idea how Santa could buzz me if I had the gizmo. But then, I had no idea how it'd made Tinkerbell spin himself unconscious. Or how Santa knew my name. I was going to find out, though. He'd said Book World was his territory. Book World was six blocks from here. I wondered how early it opened.

I peered out. "What time is it? Where's my dad?" I hadn't gone around the city much by myself. I'd better ask if it was all right with him.

"He's at work! It's ten o'clock, Lukey! Even Phoebe's out! It's just us chickens!"

At least I'd avoided Phoebe. "Where's Calvin?"

"Waiting for you, dearie! We're all waiting for you!"

"Okay." Gladys was not somebody to argue with—more like Miss Piggy than a chicken. Frilly yet ferocious. "Just give me a minute," I said. "I'll be right out."

There was a sign in the bathroom. TOUCH NOTHING. LUCAS, THIS MEANS YOU!

So much for DTIP. I washed up, dressed, put the gizmo in my pocket, and headed to the kitchen.

As I got close a nasty smell hit me. Calvin was in his high chair eating a slice of cheese. He gave me a big, woofing hello. I didn't know how anyone could eat with that stench. "What is that?" I asked Gladys, who was standing at the stove.

"I'm boiling up a pot of kidneys for Tinkie's lunch!" she said. "Tinkie's such a hungie boy today! I'll bet you're hungie too! How does oatmeal sound?"

Not good with kidneys. I was extremely hungry, but I backed away. "That's okay."

"Well, then"—I could see her checking out my hair—"you can keep an eye on the kidneys while I call Trims for Tykes. Mrs. Graham said I should take you for a haircut this morning."

"Haircut?" I backed away more. "No, thanks. I don't really—"

Bzzzzzzzzzzzzzzzzzzzzt!

If Gladys heard that, she ignored it. "I told her I'd be happy to cut your hair myself—"

"Uh, that's okay. I have something to do this morning." Hands that had touched kidneys were not touching my hair.

My hand was on the gizmo.

"Well, all I know is Mrs. Graham said I should call Trims for Tykes, and do it good and early to make sure they fit you in. She wants you to look respectable for Christmas because her family is coming and they've never met you. . . ."

My finger moved toward the remote-control whirler knob. Not that I'd ever do it.

"I have to go out," I said.

"Without your breakfast?" She looked horrified.

"I'm going to Book World," I said.

"Ooh!" She clapped her hands. "Calvin loves Book World, don't you Calvin!"

"Roof!" Calvin clapped too. "Roof, roof!"

On the other hand, Tinkerbell had loved his whirling. And he was fine now. It would be interesting to see if it worked only on cats. . . .

No. Bad idea. I'd never do it.

"See?" she said. "If you wait till these kidneys are done, we'll come with you! Calvin's been wanting to go to story hour. First we'll go to Trims for Tykes and get you a nice haircut . . ."

Maybe one small turn. Just out of scientific curiosity.

I'd barely touched the knob when Gladys let out a shriek and leaped in the air. Her head whipped around. "Goodness gracious!"

"What?" I said. "What happened?"

Before she could answer, a cockroach climbed out of the sink and walked across the counter. She ran to the stove, grabbed the wooden spoon from the kidney pot, and whacked the roach flat. Kidney juice sprayed everywhere.

Bee-bee-bee-beeeee-BLAT! Bee-bee-bee-beeeee-BLAT! The gizmo was beeping out "La Cucaracha"!

I ran to my room, threw some books in my backpack, hid the gizmo under them, and without calling Dad to see if it was okay, or saying good-bye to Calvin, I left.

It was sleeting. The sleet felt like needles on my face. I lost four quarters in four different pay phones before I found one that worked. "Dad, I'm calling you from the street," I said as soon as he picked up.

"You sound out of breath," he said. "Lucas, is something wrong?"

I'd just escaped a crazed old lady who thought I was three and wanted to lop off my hair. I had a bizarre device in my backpack and a bizarre Santa Claus sending me urgent messages. . . .

"I'm going to Book World," I said.

"Christmas shopping?" he said. "That's very enterprising of you. You've got enough money?"

A guy in a green coat walked by. "Pay phone problems, do you read me?" he said into his walkie-talkie. "Request removal authorization ASAP."

Dad was giving me instructions for getting to Book World, which I didn't need, asking me how long I planned to stay, which I didn't know. "Dad, I have to get going."

I saw more guys with green coats and walkie-talkies before I got there. And when I stopped to buy myself some snacks, the lady who sold them to me had a green coat and a walkie-talkie. Luckily, she didn't seem to know I had the gizmo. None of them did. But then, it hadn't made a peep since I'd left the apartment.

I saw two more walkie-talkie guys outside Book World. "Have a good one," they told everyone going into the store. "Have a nice day," they said to everyone going out. A lot of people were going in and out. Most of them were too busy juggling packages, zipping their coats, and struggling with umbrellas to answer.

I always got that candy store rush when I walked into a bookstore, especially when I had money in my pocket. Now, however, I was on a mission. The store was huge—three floors—and jam-packed. People crowded around every rack and display table. The checkout line was so big they had a guy directing traffic. "Step up!" he called. "Next! That's you, miss! Sir, sir, that rope is here for a reason!" There were people leaning against the walls reading, reading on the balcony stairs, on the floor, in every corner. None of them had on a Santa suit.

I walked up and down all the aisles. I checked the café at the back of the first floor. I scanned the balcony. Then I took the escalator to the top floor.

On one side of the top floor was the children's section. I could see why Calvin liked coming here. It looked so inviting. I didn't let myself browse, though. The bargain tables had tons of books I'd have loved to read. So did Sci Fi, but I kept going. I checked every aisle of the literature section—and there were dozens. I checked the men's room. I didn't know where Santa was, but he sure wasn't here.

My feet were still cold. One shoe was soaked from stepping in a puddle on the way over. I walked around till I found an empty table, sat down, and took my shoe off. I was really hungry. I unzipped my backpack and pulled out my food. I was just trying to bite my bag of chips open when an old man plunked himself in the chair across from me.

He reached over the table, grabbed the bag out of my mouth, ripped it with his own teeth, and passed it back to me. "Is it my imagination?" he said. "Or is New York City getting more and more annoying?"

CHAPTER 4

He wasn't wearing a Santa suit. He had a rusty blackish brown toupee, a shiny green sport jacket, and a gray-and-purple-striped tie. But the voice was unmistakable.

"Because if you ask me," he said, "which you didn't, the annoyance factor is through the roof."

"You can say that again!" I said.

"And no doubt will." He picked up the candy bar I'd bought from the walkie-talkie lady. "Stars Bar Lite, eh? You realize why it has one third less calories. Because it's one third smaller. Same great big wrapper, new teeny tiny bar. And would you mind telling me why they spell it *L-i-t-e*?"

I laughed. "Santa?"

"Don't be ridiculous." He unwrapped the Stars Bar and took a bite. "A red suit and a pillow doth not a Santa make. I only wear it when HQ insists."

I handed him the gizmo. He studied it. "Ah, yes! I knew you were the man for the job."

"Why? What is it?" I said. "What does it do?"

"Inspects, detects, protects, corrects. And possibly other things as well, but that's a conversation for another time.

As is our talk about annoyance levels." He stood up and leaned across the table. His breath smelled like Juicy Fruit. His coat smelled like a sheep. His mustache looked glued on. "I've got agents treading on my toes, nipping at my heels, undoing my work faster than I can do it—" *Bzzzzzzzzzzzzzzzzzt!* The gizmo went off. "See what I mean?"

"What's up with this buzzing?" I said.

"It's the call to duty." He looked at it and pressed more buttons. "*Hasta la* bye-bye, my friend! Gotta hop! Put your shoe on," he called, helping himself to a chip before he disappeared around a bookcase. "Or you'll be hopping too."

I did, then grabbed my things and tried to follow him, but there were too many aisles, too many corners, too many nooks and crannies, too many tables with books piled too high to see over.

I couldn't lose him now. I'd just found him.

Then I heard *Beedle-dee-BEEP-bee-beeeeep!* coming from the children's section. I headed over there. A few minutes ago it was crowded but cheerful. Now half the kids were crying, the other half were whining, and all the grown-ups looked grouchy. I saw several guys with green coats carrying clipboards and heard somebody whistling "Grandma Got Run Over by a Reindeer," but I didn't see the old man.

Beep-BEE-bee-dee-BEE-bee-dee-BEEEE!

Okay. He was here somewhere.

Bee-BEE-bee-BEEDLE-dee-BEEE-BLEEP!

"Be Kind to Your Web-Footed Friends"; "The Bear Went Over the Mountain"; "La Cucaracha." How many songs did this gizmo play?

"Excuse me. Excuse me. May I get through, please?" I stepped over people's legs and around strollers, teddy bears, snowsuits, books, and parkas.

"Excuse *you!*" said a large lady in a green coat. She looked like Santa's friend Hildegund.

"Sorry." I skirted around a little boy lying in the aisle, kicking his legs and howling as his father begged him to calm down so they could get his jacket on.

The whistling got louder—crazy warbling, like a hyper canary. It was "I Saw Mommy Kissing Santa Claus" now, and it was the old man. He walked down one aisle, up another, whistling so hard, his mustache wobbled. He looked so funny. No one was laughing, though. No one seemed to notice. Except that every aisle he went down, the whining and crying stopped. The grown-ups no longer looked frazzled. Some were even smiling. "Thank goodness!" the dad sighed as the little boy stopped howling.

The old man came up behind me. "So am I good, or am I good?"

"If you did that," I said, "you're amazing."

"Piece of cake," he said. "You learn it in Abatement 101. Hard on the lips, but it works like a charm. Uh-oh." The little boy had started throwing a fit again. A lot of kids had started throwing fits again. "I'd stay and chat, but these agents are not helping me. Why are they even here? That's what I want to know." He adjusted his toupee and, with the gizmo in his hand, walked off whistling "Jingle Bell Rock."

I stood there watching as he whistled it over and over. He almost had the children's section under control when— *Beep-BEE-bee-dee-BEE-bee-dee-BEEEE!*—the gizmo went off again. He checked it and, still whistling, trotted toward the escalator.

I couldn't wait to see what he was going to do next.

"Step aside, kiddo. You're blocking traffic." He jumped onto the up escalator and began running down. I got on the down escalator. "Watch your back, madam. Pardon me.

Move it, mister. Coming through. This is business here. Official business. Hold on to the railing, young lady! Miss, you're gonna hurt yourself reading on the escalator."

He hopped off at the second floor. "Sir, what are you doing?" he shouted to someone on the balcony. "Yeah, you. Cut that out!" He elbowed past shoppers, stopping briefly to pick up a kid's mitten and help a woman fold her stroller. "I said, coming through!" He stepped around some teenagers sitting on the balcony stairs and ran to Puzzles, where a tall, preppy, elderly guy was shoving a book back on the shelf. By the time I was up the stairs, Santa had his finger in the guy's chest.

"You do the puzzles, you buy the book!" he scolded. "You do not put it back. Shame on you! And in pen, no less." He grabbed the book from the shelf and stuck it in the guy's hand. "It's yours now, buddy. Go pay for it."

"But, but . . . " Mr. Preppy sputtered. Mr. Preppy's face was so red, I'd have felt bad if he hadn't looked exactly like Mr. Grant, the Bentley headmaster. "I've never done anything like this before. No, I mean it this time. It won't happen again." He ran down the stairs.

Bzzzzt! The gizmo went off again.

The old man checked it. "Oy, oy, oy! No rest for the weary!" He hurried on down the balcony. I ran after him. "Not to boast, sonny boy, but this device is remarkable! You think the fax machine was life changing? Velcro? The Ziploc bag? Those antediluvian, bureaucratic, nay-saying so-called colleagues of mine can scoff all they want! Mark my words! Once this baby's up and running, the world will never be the same! Speaking of Ziploc bags . . ." He took one from his pocket.

"Now what are you doing? What are you talking about?" I said. "I don't get this. Who are you? And who are these agents?"

He leaned down, looked under a table, took a pair of long tweezers from his pocket, pulled off a big pink wad of gum, and dropped it in the bag, which, I could see, already contained blobs of all different colors.

"What are you doing now?" I called as he walked farther and stopped in front of a display rack.

"Hey," he said. "Has anyone told you that constant questions can be exceedingly annoying? I mean that in the best possible way, of course. And coming from me, it's a compliment." He pulled out a book. "Hell's bells! They'll publish anything these days! Look at this! *Overcoming the Annoying Habits That Wreck Homes and Destroy Your Peace of Mind.* Here's another! *Annoying Habits Can Be Overcome.* Overcome, my aunt Fanny! What, are they living in dreamland? Good thing I'm here!" He took a Post-it pad from his pocket and stuck one on the rack. The note had a circle with a red *X* through it and the letters ABGNY. "You've got to nip these things in the bud. Today's two is tomorrow's ten. One being mildly irksome, ten being insufferably pestiferous. Like, to choose something at random, the smell of kidneys."

He knew about that?

"Should I be getting scared?" I asked.

"Only if you insist," he said. "There are scarier things. At least to my mind." He was peering over the balcony railing to the main floor.

Gladys was waving up at me. "Lukey! There you are! See, Calvin, there's Lukey! Say 'Hi, Lukey'!" Calvin barked, and bounced in his stroller. "I told you we'd find him!"

"Gotta hop!" the old man said.

"Wait. Where are you going?" He couldn't leave now. He couldn't leave me with her.

"So many annoyances," he said. "So little time. I'll be back." And he trotted off down the balcony.

"Well," Gladys said once I was downstairs. "I called Trims for Tykes, but they just couldn't fit you in today. I begged and pleaded—"

"That's okay. It's fine. Really." Her voice was so loud. Her coat was so pink. Good thing there was no one here I knew. I was glad no one here knew me. I looked up at the balcony.

"So I made you an appointment for Monday, called Mrs. Graham and told her we'd be coming here for story hour, and here we are!" She checked her watch. "And right on time, too! It's about to start! Calvin says goody gumdrops, don't you, Calvin!"

"Woof! Woof! Woof!" At least Calvin looked happy.

She folded the stroller and we took the escalator to the children's section, where fifteen or twenty little kids were already sitting in a circle on the floor around a lady in a Santa hat. With a loud "Oooof!" Gladys sat down and put Calvin on her lap. I sat next to them. I was the only kid over six.

The story lady read a Hanukkah story, a Kwanza story, and a Christmas story. At least that's what she announced. I was too busy trying to spot the old man to pay attention. I kept hearing the crackle of walkie-talkies. I watched a lady agent walk around with a big black lawn-and-leaf bag, picking up toys and stuffed animals off the floor. She walked from stroller to stroller, muttering about crumbs everywhere and annoying crunching noises disturbing readers, removing things from people's stroller bags. "Nibble patrol complete," I heard her say into her walkie-talkie. "Annoying items duly confiscated. Over." I watched an agent roust people from the armchairs they were reading in, then load the chairs onto a hand truck and wheel them to an elevator. Then I watched two more agents bring in folding plastic chairs instead. "Loitering abatement in process," I heard one say into his walkie-talkie. I was sure the old man would come bounding over to stop them, but I didn't see him, and I didn't hear any beeps or buzzes. And as usual, nobody but me seemed to think anything strange was going on. Or maybe they were all too busy to notice.

I was amazed how much Calvin enjoyed the stories. He sat in Gladys's lap listening for a long time. Then he got up and climbed into his stroller and listened from there. Then he turned around and started fishing in the stroller bag. "Calvin, are you hungie?" Gladys whispered to him. He barked. "Would you like some juicey?" Her whisper was no softer than his barking.

"Shhh!" another little kid's mom said, leaning toward her.

"Grrrrr!" Calvin growled at the lady. Then he started whining.

"Would you like your animal crackers?" Gladys whispered to him.

"Woof! Woof, woof!"

"Shhh! Other children are trying to listen," the mom scolded.

"Push the stroller over for me, and I'll get them for you," Gladys whispered.

I stood up. "I'll get them."

Except for a diaper, the stroller bag was empty. I whispered that to Gladys.

"That can't be!" she said. "Check again!"

Calvin checked with me, then started to whine louder. Other people were shushing us now. "Sorry," I told them. "There's nothing in here," I told Gladys.

"There's no animal crackers? What about the peanut butter sandwiches and the juice boxes! And the bag of Cheerios! I put them there right before we left! Oooof!" She got up, came over, and looked too. "Where could they have gone?"

I knew exactly where they'd gone. They were in the agent's lawn-and-leaf bag. And now she'd gone.

Calvin started crying, which seemed to start a trend. Within seconds every little kid had jumped up and started rummaging through their stroller bags, their diaper bags, their moms' purses. Everyone's snacks must have been gone. Pretty soon so many kids were crying, the poor story lady had to stop reading.

"Come on, boys," Gladys said, taking Calvin's hand. "We'll have our lunch at home."

"I'm going to stay here for a while, if it's all right," I told her.

No way was I leaving without finding out what all this was about.

"What it's about," the old man said, "is fossilized functionaries who think they've got the answers! Who, under the delusion that they're helping, are making my world even more annoying than before!" He'd appeared almost as soon as Gladys and Calvin left. He had the Santa suit on again. I told him what had happened. "And here I thought I was only giving you a quick annoyance overview," he said. "The briefest intro, a little flavor. Instead, willy-nilly, you are plunged up to the eyeballs in the full panoply of annoyances. Not that this should surprise you. It's clear you have an up close and personal acquaintance with the subject. The world, as we both know, Lucas, is a staggeringly annoying place. The question is what you do about it. I do what I can—about what I can. And we're going to do more, you and I. You bet your bippy!"

CHAPTER 5

There were loud giggles coming from Phoebe's room when I got home. Dad was back from work. He and Calvin were taking a bath. "Come in, Lucas!" Phoebe sang.

Why I obeyed, I'll never know, unless it was the excitement at Book World wiping out all memory of last night. I'd stayed at the store almost the whole day. I didn't see any more of the old man—he went back to Santa duty—but I'd found a big, comfortable armchair the agents hadn't removed and sat reading and looking out for agents. Book World might be staggeringly annoying to the old man. I loved it.

Phoebe and two other girls were sitting on her bed listening to music and cutting pictures from magazines. "This is Zoë and this is Chloe," Phoebe said. She didn't say which was which. They looked kind of alike: thin, ponytail, braces, makeup. They looked kind of like her.

"Hey," they said.

"Hey," I said. My voice came out higher than I'd hoped.

"So, Lucas," Phoebe stopped giggling long enough to say. "Have you been to the bathroom yet?"

"No. Why?" I wondered if I looked like I had to go, or if this was something to do with the beauty products.

Actually, I did have to go. Not with them there, though. I went down the hall to Dad and Claire's bathroom. Dad and Calvin were still in the tub. "This old man, he played one . . ." Dad used to sing that to me all the time in the bathtub when I was little. I could remember chortling just like Calvin was doing.

When I returned to my room, there was a sign taped to my side of the bathroom door.

OCCUPIED. OCUPADO. OCCUPÉ. STAY OUT.

I could hear the girls inside, laughing. I knocked. "Excuse me. Think I can get in there, please?"

"We're giving ourselves makeovers," Phoebe called. "We could give you one." They all giggled.

"Uh, how long is that going to take?"

"To do you? Hours? Days? Years? Millennia?"

"And otherwise you'll be out when?"

"No clue. And would you mind not cracking your knuckles? We can hear it through the door."

Not unless she had superpowers. But I stopped cracking them and tried Dad's bathroom again. Dad and Calvin were still in there.

"This old man, he played eleven, he played—no, Calvin. No! Calvin, not in the bath! Calvin, Daddy's not going to want to take any more baths with you if . . . okay, Calvin! That's it! Bath's over!"

I had never done that to him. But now I really had to go. I headed for the little bathroom off the kitchen. Tinkerbell was in his litter box. He stopped scratching, looked up at me, and hissed.

And the old man thought Book World was annoying?

We waited for dinner till Claire came home from shopping. I'd hoped Phoebe's friends would have left by then.

"It's so nice to have all you kids here at the table," Claire said, nibbling an asparagus spear. "It feels like a Christmas party. Which reminds me. Lucas, I'm so happy Gladys got you that hair appointment for Monday. I wanted to take care of it today, so I'd have one less detail to worry about—"

"You didn't have to worry about it," I said.

Five people stared at my head like, *That's what you think!*

Save me, Dad. Tell Claire my hair's good the way it is.

I seemed to be the only person in the world who liked my hair.

Phoebe said something in French. Her friends laughed.

"Claire, isn't there another haircut place I can go to besides . . ." No way was I saying "Trims for Tykes" in front of Phoebe and her friends.

Phoebe spoke French again and, when Claire wasn't looking, made snipping motions with her fingers. Her friends laughed harder.

Ignore them, I told myself. All I'd had to eat today was the Stars Bar, a Snapple, the chips, and a bigger, nonlite candy bar I'd bought from a different, non-walkie-talkie-guy newsstand on the way home. The chicken was good. The potato was very good. The asparagus—I ignored the asparagus. I could feel the girls' eyes on me every time I took a bite of chicken. I could see them watching my Adam's apple each time I took a sip of milk. I tried to swallow without it bobbling up and down. They giggled harder.

"Ooh, Charles, this asparagus is great!" Claire said.

"It is, isn't it?" Dad said.

I have a problem with asparagus, even little skinny ones. These were like mini flashlights. Claire had put five of them on my plate. Mom and Dad had always made me try everything. Even if I knew I hated it, I still had to taste. I didn't want Dad to think I'd turned into a wimp, especially because Calvin was chomping his down happily. I didn't want to be like my friend Dan's guinea pig—afraid of his food.

I managed to choke down one whole asparagus spear without breathing. So why, when I looked at my plate again, did I now have eight of them? This didn't feel like the mysteries at Book World. This felt like Phoebe.

She was sitting there, innocently peeling the skin off her chicken and feeding it to Tinkerbell, under the table. I waited till everyone was talking, palmed an asparagus spear, and held it out to him. I could feel him sniff it. He took it. Hmmm. I might need to re-think Tinkerbell. I gave him another. Two down, six to go.

Phoebe said something else in French, which once again her friends found hilarious.

Claire frowned.

"I'm glad you ladies are finding dinner so entertaining," Dad said. "Unfortunately some of us don't happen to speak French. You're taking Spanish, right, Lucas?"

"Yeah," I said.

They laughed harder.

"I was talking to Mother, Dad," Phoebe said. "Asking her to please remind Lucas that there's no feeding Tinkerbell at the table."

"She's right, Lucas," Claire said. "It's one of our rules. It would set a bad example for Calvin."

This time when I swallowed, I didn't care if they could see my Adam's apple. An up close and personal acquaintance with annoyance, Santa had said? This was too up close and way too personal. "Dad? Claire?" I said. "I need to be excused."

I went to my room and ripped down Phoebe's STAY OUT sign. At least I had the bathroom to myself.

Except I didn't. She'd put signs in the bathroom now, too, in fluorescent markers, each letter a different color:

LEAVE TOILET SEAT DOWN
↓
Your towel
↓
Not your towel
↓
Hairs in the
sink stink!

What was it Santa had said about being up to the eyeballs?

"Those things you said yesterday, about staggeringly annoying?" I told the old man the next morning. "You were right."

I'd talked Dad and Claire into letting me go to Book World as soon as I finished breakfast. I told them I'd started the most amazing fantasy adventure book there yesterday, and that I'd go berserk if I couldn't go right back and finish it. I also assured them the store opened at nine on Sunday mornings, when in fact I didn't know if it was open at all. Or if the old man would be there.

This was not like me. On the other hand, it got me out of the apartment before Phoebe woke up. I wouldn't have to see her till noon, when Dad was going to pick me up and we'd all meet for brunch.

The store was open. I spotted the old man as soon as I stepped off the escalator. He was in the cookbook section, sticking a Post-it on a book called *Banana Mutt Bars, Birdy Biscuits, and Other Howl-iday Pet Treats.*

"The annoyance factor is through the roof!" I said.

"And getting worse," he said. "Good morning, Lucas." He

didn't look surprised to see me. "I prayed there'd be no agents here today. I prayed they'd give it up. This is three days in a row now. This does not bode well."

"Well, it's only my second full day, and I'm totally annoyed," I said.

Beedle-beep-beep-BEEDLE-beedle-beedle-deedle! The gizmo went off. He took it out of his pocket and looked it over.

"Quick! Get down!" He pulled me over to an armchair a few feet away. We crouched behind it.

"What's up?" I whispered.

"It's Agent Bramble." He put his hand over my mouth. It smelled like fishy onions. I tried not to breathe. A minute later a lady with a lawn-and-leaf bag and a clipboard walked by. "Seventy-nine, eighty, eighty-one," I heard her say.

"Oh, they do love collecting data," he whispered. "They'll collect and count, and count and measure, they'll graph and chart till the cows come home—"

The gizmo began to buzz. He pressed a button. "We'd better kill the sound before we tip them off. I'm going to need your help here, Lucas."

"Doing what?" I said.

He pointed toward the restrooms. The agent was handing her bag and clipboard to someone inside.

"You'll be my eyes and ears. You'll walk in, take a quick gander, then come back and give me a report."

"Uh . . ." This felt a little scary.

"Don't worry, Lucas. Believe me, they're so wrapped up in their work . . ."

I went over to the men's room, opened the door, and peeked in.

Two agents sat cross-legged on the floor. The first guy—it looked like the weaselly one from the other night—had a mountain of snack foods in front of him, some in bags and boxes, some loose on the floor, and one of those big, old-fashioned file folders with a compartment for each letter of the alphabet. Each time he put something in a compartment, he called out the name, and the big, lumpy one wrote on his clipboard. "Fig Newton, check. Vienna Finger, check. Chips Ahoy!, oatmeal raisin, Girl Scout—check. Moving on to chip items. Nacho cheese, check. Guiltless low salt . . ."

The old man was right. They had no clue I was watching them. I walked in.

"Do animal crackers go under Cookies or Crackers?" Lumpy asked.

Animal crackers? Wait till the old man heard this! I sneaked into a stall and shut the door.

"Eyeballing these numbers," I heard, "there appears to be a fourteen percent increase in the Cheerios take over last week at this time. Nine thousand and three, to be exact."

Then, "That's one form done. Three more to go before our break."

Then, "Roger that. Let's knock off children next."

What? I jumped up on the toilet and peered over the stall door.

"I'll read this time. You log," Lumpy was saying. "Saturday totals: Criers, forty-seven. Whiners, two hundred thirteen. Dirty diapers, six hundred eleven. Hissy fits, twenty. Temper tantrums, three full-blown, two incipient. On to mothers."

"I thought we did caregivers first," Weaselly said.

"They changed the form. Mothers. You ready? Irritable, thirty-two. Testy, ninety-three. Wit's end, twenty-six. Hmmph. Sounds low . . ."

"Refresh my memory. The exact definition of 'wit's end' again?" Weaselly looked at his watch. "Never mind. Break time!" They stashed the clipboards and pens under the radiator, grabbed their folder, stood up, and went out.

I waited a second, then went out after them. The old man was still behind the chair. I squatted next to him. "You were right! They were in there counting things! Not only that . . . look!" I pointed toward the gardening section. "There they are again!" Weaselly and Lumpy had sat down at a table and were taking things from their file folder and eating them. "They're eating their evidence!" I watched as Weaselly pulled out a box of animal crackers. "I'll bet you anything those are my little brother's crackers. They take little kids' crackers, and then they wonder why things aren't going well in the children's section? That makes no sense!"

"My point precisely!" The old man was beaming at me. "Their heads are screwed on backward. You, on the other hand . . ." He clapped me on the shoulder. "You, my friend, just said a mouthful. Those snacks are the only thing keeping toddler annoyance levels under control."

"Who are these guys?" I said.

He snorted. "My so-called colleagues. My coworkers. My fellow bureau members. That runty-looking specimen"—he nodded toward Weaselly, who was cramming Calvin's crackers in his mouth as fast as he could—"is Agent Casimir Pellet, from Operations. The rotund gentleman is Agent Tuber, Vivian J., from Resource Recovery, and yonder dude"—he pointed to a tall, skinny guy with beady eyes, black-rimmed glasses, and a strip of beard down the middle of his chin— "is Elpidio Zapp. Audit and Control. I don't doubt Pandora Bramble is around too, but I don't see her at the moment. And now that I've acquainted you with them," he said, standing up, "the only agent left to introduce is *moi*." He stuck his hand out. "Izzy Gribitz. Annoyance Bureau. Outreach Division. Let's go somewhere and talk."

CHAPTER
6

Izzy led me to the far end of the floor and around a corner to an elevator, and pressed the button. The elevator door opened. "After you."

"I don't get this at all," I told him.

"You're not expected to get it," he said. "How could you get it? It's highly complex. It's ever changing—"

"Sometimes people see you and sometimes they can't," I said. "How does this work?"

He was still holding the elevator button. "Think about it, Lucas. 'Agent, Agent, come quickly! My toilet's stopped up!' 'Agent, I need you! My wife's driving me bats!' 'Get over here, Agent, the fax has a paper jam.' No. We can be noticed when we want to be. The rest of the time we operate below the radar."

I was still standing there. "So then why do I see them all? Why do I see you?"

"Aha! Now, there's an interesting question," he said.

I got in. He pressed *B*. The elevator went down. And down. And down some more, until finally the door opened, and we stepped out into a long hallway that smelled like sauerkraut. "Where are we? Where are we going?" I said as we walked past several closed doors.

"Right here. Where nobody will bother us," he said, opening the door to a large, windowless room with green lockers along one wall, a watercooler, an exercise bike, weights, and equipment like the kind advertised on late-night TV. Abdomenizer. Glute Master. Thigh Blaster. "Agents are supposed to stay in shape, but—what a surprise—they don't. Here you go." He pulled two large plastic exercise balls over to a metal table. "Take a load off."

I checked my watch. I had an hour before I was supposed to meet Dad outside the store so we could join Claire, Calvin, and Phoebe for brunch. I sat down on a ball.

He went to a locker and came back with a large sack, straddled the other ball, and ripped the sack open. "Care for a nut?" he said, pouring a pile of pistachio nuts onto the table. "Dig in."

"Uh, no thank you." I couldn't have eaten them even if I'd wanted. The shells were tightly closed.

"We got these in the last annoyance sweep," he said. "Annoying, isn't it? Almost as annoying as that red dye that comes off on your fingers. Which brings us to the subject at hand. The Annoyance Bureau."

"Why don't you have a walkie-talkie?" I said. "The other guys all have them."

"The other guys need walkie-talkies. They're schleppers." He raised his eyebrows. "Lucas, are you going to pepper me with questions, or are you going to let me talk?" He went over to a locker and came back with a stretched-out athletic sock, which he waved under my nose. "Exhibit A. From the same annoyance sweep."

"P.U.!" I turned my head away.

"That's right. It stinks," he said. "But not for long. So. You think bad smells just happen to go away after a few seconds, vanish, disappear into thin air?"

"Yes," I said. "Or our noses stop smelling them."

"Aha! We let everyone think that," he said. "But it's the Annoyance Bureau, Department of Corrections, Abatement Division. That's easy to understand, right? Now, here's where it gets more complicated. Exhibit B." He took off his glasses and pressed the earpiece. They beeped. "The beep is an extremely irritating sound, and yet each day more and more things beep at you. Who was it that declared all things must beep? Was it an act of Congress? Was it Bill Gates? You'll hear all sorts of explanations, such as that the glasses need to beep so you can find them when they fall inside the couch. And that's true. And it's good. And it improves life. But make no mistake. It's also us. The bureau. Research and Development Department."

"Wait a minute," I said. "I thought you removed annoyances."

"That's because I'm in Abatement." He went over to an exercise bike and began dusting it with the sock. "Abatement takes away. Research and Development adds. Not always, and never deliberately, but it happens. Call it an unfortunate side effect. Something annoying coming from something good." He must have seen that I was about to interrupt again. "Okay. We'll leave that aside for the moment. Exhibit C." He went back to the locker and returned with a plastic-wrapped fruitcake with a red bow on top. "You've heard fruitcake jokes, right? Everyone complains about fruitcake, saying how everyone hates fruitcake, and yet some people must like it, because fruitcake continues to get made and sold, and if all the fruitcakes in the world were suddenly to disappear, even the people who claim to hate it would start yelling, 'Where's the fruitcake? It's not Christmas without fruitcake!' Well, it's the same with annoyances. You've got to have some. It's a question of

how many. Parts of the world are seriously under¡
Whereas we, as I'm sure you'd be the first to a
overendowed. We might even say overwhelmed. ᵢₜₛ ₐₗ
balance and harmony. Distribution. Redistribution."

He climbed on the bike and started pedaling.

"Can we back up a minute?" I said. "Are you telling me
the Annoyance Bureau removes annoyances or creates
them?"

"My question exactly!" He pedaled faster. "Which is why
I'm so incensed, why I walk around in a swivet, why I've
begun this outreach!"

The door opened. The four agents stalked in.

"What outreach?" Agent Pellet demanded. "And what's
this about Outreach Division? There is no Outreach Division!"

"You're way out on a limb there, my friend!" Agent Tuber
said.

"This is totally outside the parameters!" Agent Zapp
shook his finger at him. "Refusing to turn in an unauthorized device, consorting with underage civilians. You are not
a team player, you refuse to follow procedures, you—"

"What did you expect?" The lady agent had that disap-
pointed-teacher look. "He has issues with authority. Always
has, always will."

Izzy pedaled faster. "So far these are all good things
you're telling me," he said. "So then, what's the problem?"

"You bring up this same outreach nonsense at every session," the lady agent said. "And every session we turn it
down."

"Furthermore," Agent Pellet said, "if there were an Outreach Division, it wouldn't be you. You're on your way out,
Gribby. Everyone knows that. My name's been on the pro-
motion list for fifty-three years. . . ."

Izzy pedaled with his arms folded now, waiting for them to shut up. "Gentlemen, lady, your timing is perfect," he said when they finally did. "Lucas, Exhibit D. I was trying to explain to you the Annoyance Bureau ideal. You see before you the pathetic reality." He hopped off the bike. "I see you're admiring their uniforms. What color would you call that? Bile green? Nile green? The noxious green of canned string beans in three-bean salad?" He strode over to Agent Tuber. "What are you doing down here, anyway, Vivian? Hiding from your supervisor, per usual? Because I know you can't be coming down to get fit."

"I'm not hiding!" Agent Tuber huffed. "I'm preparing my stress ball report. Did you know stress ball sales have risen one hundred thirty-eight percent—"

"Your reports are due too, Agent Gribitz! With charts and attachments, please, this time!" Agent Zapp said. "This evening. Close of business."

"My business never closes," Izzy told him. "Inspect, detect, protect, correct. That's what I do. I make things better. Unlike you. And unlike you, I'm on duty twenty-four seven. Which is why I'm too busy to chart stress ball sales and count cookies."

The four agents marched out as suddenly as they'd marched in.

"Cheerios," I told Izzy. "It wasn't just cookies. They were counting Cheerios."

"And does that make sense to you, Lucas?" he said. "Are you starting to get my drift here? Are you starting to understand why Agent Gribitz of the Annoyance Bureau of Greater New York is not a happy camper? Are you starting to get a feel for the problem? Who ever heard of an Annoyance Bureau that makes the world more annoying? What sense does that make?"

"Not a lot," I said.

"I live in hope, though," he said, walking back over to the table. "Our scope is vast. Our task is boundless. We're multi-divisional, transnational, global. We add annoyances. We take away. We multiply. We can even divide, if we feel the need. You sure you wouldn't like a nut?"

He pointed to the pistachios. A second ago every shell had been closed up tight as a clam. Now, right there in front of me, they began to open.

I couldn't believe it. "How'd you do that?"

He smiled. "That's for me to know and you, my promising young apprentice, to find out."

CHAPTER
7

"I don't think so!" I'd been going along as if this were something I was reading in a book or watching on TV. As if nuts always popped open on command, as if everyone hung out with guys who were sometimes visible, sometimes not. I jumped to my feet. "I'm outta here! I gotta go!"

"Lucas! Where are you rushing to?" Izzy shouted as I ran out the door and down the hallway to the elevator. "What's your hurry? We're just getting started here. We've barely scratched the surface."

I pressed the elevator button. Nothing happened. I pressed again. Still nothing. Oh, no! There was a sign next to the elevator: OUT OF ORDER.

"Hold on, Lucas, I wasn't going to introduce you to that yet," Izzy called after me as I began to run. "On the other hand, if you insist . . ."

I kept running. The corridor joined up with a wider one, wider than a city sidewalk—more like an underground road, an old road, with tiled walls and a tile ceiling. It had no windows and no exit signs that I could see. It wasn't a subway tunnel; I'd been in the subway. It was way too big for a basement, even the basement of a megastore. It looked like it could go for miles. It looked deserted.

I ran on. There were no more doors now, and still no exit signs. No signs at all. The smell had changed from sauerkraut to flowers, but I didn't see any flowers. Now that Izzy had stopped calling to me, except for my feet pounding on the cobblestones, it was silent. Then I heard maniacal laughter, horrible fun-house giggling, coming from a side corridor up ahead.

The laughter grew louder. I was wondering if I should turn around when a man in a green Annoyance Bureau coat, ear protectors, and reflector sunglasses trudged out of the side corridor pushing a wheelbarrow. His wheelbarrow was loaded with Tickle Me Elmo dolls.

Whew! I stopped. "Excuse me! Sir?" I couldn't see his eyes at all.

He set down the wheelbarrow and took off his ear protectors.

"I need to get back to Book World!" I had to scream to be heard over the cackling, snickering dolls.

"A few more blocks. You can't miss it," he shouted, pointing straight ahead.

That wasn't right. The tiles in front of us were blue, like a swimming pool. I hadn't been through any blue corridors. "You're sure it's up ahead?" I said. "I came from back there, and it was right upstairs. It's not right upstairs?"

"No, sirree!" He put his ear protectors back on, picked up the handles of the wheelbarrow, and kept going.

I kept running. The walls in this section were damp, and there was mossy green stuff hanging from the ceiling. I could hear water dripping and what sounded like ducks quacking. Another Annoyance Bureau guy was coming toward me. He had on the same dark glasses as the first one. His cart was filled with plaid pants. The labels all said the same thing: 58 SHORT.

I stopped. "Sir, I'm trying to find Book World," I told him.

"Yeah, well, you're going the wrong way." He pointed in the direction I'd just come. "It's that way. About three miles. You can't miss it."

Three miles? No way had I run three miles. "You're sure?"

"You asked me. I'm telling you."

A man driving a forklift loaded with boxes labeled FAT-FREE IMITATION DIET CHEESE FOOD stopped alongside me. He had on the same Annoyance Bureau outfit and the same glasses. "Yo, yo. Whatchu looking for?"

"Book World. Please!"

He pointed down a side corridor whose walls were covered with orange shag carpeting. There was a strong orangy smell, like Kool-Aid or children's aspirin.

I knew that wasn't right.

"Book World? Nah! You wanna go that way!" A man lugging a basket full of snarled, kinked telephone cords pointed in the opposite direction.

A guy driving a golf cart with boxes marked APHIDS, THRIPS, MEALWORMS, MEALYBUGS, CHIGGERS, NEMATODES. DO NOT OPEN! pointed straight ahead and yelled something to me in what sounded like Hungarian.

"Listen. I have to find Book World!" I begged a man with a wheelbarrow full of signs: PUSH. PULL. CONTENTS UNDER PRESSURE. ENTRADA PROHIBIDA. WET PAINT. BUMP. ONE WAY. SLIPPERY WHEN WET. NO HOT WATER. RESTROOM FOR CUS-TOMER USE ONLY. NO PARKING. DO NOT ENTER. LOT FULL. SOLD OUT. NO LEFT TURN. BUS STOPS HERE. CANCELED TILL

FURTHER NOTICE. CLOSED FOR REPAIRS. CLOSED FOR LUNCH. CLOSED FOR VACATION. SORRY, WE'RE CLOSED.

"I have to find it fast! Please!" Dad would go nuts if I wasn't outside at noon. And then if he went in Book World and couldn't find me . . .

"If you want fast, don't *go* there," the man said. "This is the twenty-first century, bubba. Order books online."

"What?" I had a stitch in my side. Sweat was blurring up my eyes. More carts rolled by carrying platform shoes, lavender clothes, VCRs, huge ladies' pocketbooks, cages of parakeets. There was a strong smell of skunk.

I sat down on a pile of boxes. On the other side of the passage was another pile. I could see now that the boxes were labeled. OVERCOMING THE ANNOYING HABITS THAT WRECK HOMES AND DESTROY YOUR PEACE OF MIND. ANNOYING HABITS CAN BE OVERCOME. BANANA MUTT BARS, BIRDY BISCUITS, AND OTHER HOWL-IDAY PET TREATS.

The same titles Santa had shown me in Book World! My heart started pounding.

"Hey, kid. I'm tryin' to make a pickup here. Would you mind movin' over?" A short, fat man stopped his golf cart next to me, got out, and began loading up the books.

"Where are you taking them?" I asked.

"Bookstores," he said. "Brooklyn."

"Brooklyn? This goes all the way to Brooklyn?" I knew Brooklyn was far away.

"Oh, yeah. Brooklyn, Queens, the Bronx, Jersey City, you name it. Anywhere you wanna go."

"You know Book World?" I asked him. "The store these books came from? Can you tell me where that is?"

Please.

"Sorry, pal," he said. "No clue."

But as soon as he'd loaded up the last box, I saw that

they'd been stacked in front of a door. I pushed against it. It opened, and I saw stairs!

It wasn't till I'd raced up the first flight that I realized I'd let the door slam without making sure I could open it from the inside. I ran up another flight. And another and another, till I got to another door. I opened it. And almost cried.

It wasn't Book World. I was in some kind of storeroom lined with metal shelves filled with sacks of rice, cans of tomatoes, boxes of noodles. I could hear bangs and clangs, hisses, water running, people shouting. At the far end of the room was a swinging door.

I opened it and stepped out into a restaurant full of people. I'd barely taken three steps when over the clank of dishes and the hum of voices I heard, "Woof! Woof, woof!"

Calvin?

"You can have one, honey. But you need to ask for it. You can say bis-*cot*-ti. Barking is not the way to get what you want."

Claire?

"Lucas?" Claire looked somewhat surprised but smiled as I went over to her table. She moved her shopping bags so I could sit. Calvin was in a baby seat. He woofed me a hello. "I thought you were meeting your dad at the bookstore," she said.

"I know. Right." My brain was whirling faster than Tink with the whirler button. I had to come up with a story. "Uh . . ."

She took out her cell phone. "Charles, Lucas seems to have been a bit confused about the arrangements," she told Dad. "He's here with us. Yes. I know. I know. Just come on over." When she hung up, she said, "Don't worry about it, Lucas. These things happen. You got distracted." She reached across to pat down my hair. "I hope you had a good morning."

I had no way to answer that.

Luckily, the waiter came over. "How're you folks doing this morning? I'm Justin, your server. May I tell you about our specials? Chef Lionel makes an extraordinary egg white omelette with imported wild forest mushrooms and shaved truffles—"

"I've had it. It's excellent!" Claire smiled up at him. "And Calvin's crazy about your roasted root vegetable frittata. I'd love a skim milk latte with a shot of foam while we wait. But you'll need to give us a minute, Justin, please. My husband and daughter should be along momentarily."

"No problemo," Justin said.

Somewhere in here Phoebe came; Dad arrived; we ordered and ate our brunch. I doubt I ate truffles or roasted roots, but beyond that, I have no idea. They might all have been speaking Hungarian. Or Martian. Or Gribitzian.

Until I heard Phoebe say, "Lucas is so quiet. Do you think he has a secret life? The secret life of Lucas Graham? Except what would that be? Unless maybe he has a girl-friend. That could explain why he's so silent and mysteri-ous." She leaned toward me. "Lucas, are you in love?"

Claire frowned at her. "Lucas," she said. "We were just discussing Phoebe's plans for the rest of the day. She's meet-ing Chloe and Zoë, and they're going to walk around the West Side—"

"Mother." Phoebe did her slump-sigh.

"What?" Claire said. "I thought you girls were into boys."

"Yes. That's boys as in . . . boys. Not boys as in—"

"We'll discuss that another time," Claire said. "You girls can certainly include Lucas in your shopping." She turned to me. "You haven't finished your Christmas shopping yet, have you, Lucas?" She gave Phoebe a don't-say-a-word look. "If you'd like to join Phoebe and her friends . . ."

Fortunately for me, Dad said he needed to get home and check his e-mail, so I went with him.

"You're awfully subdued, Lucas," Dad said as we walked.

"Sorry," I said. It was all I could do to keep from blurting out at least some of what had happened, but there was no way to say it that didn't make me sound as if I'd lost my mind.

"So did you finish that fantasy adventure whatever you were so engrossed in?" he asked. "I'm assuming that's why the arrangements mix-up . . ."

"Uh, yeah. No."

"Well, tomorrow's another day," he said. "You can go back tomorrow."

I went to my room as soon as we got home, to try to make sense of what had happened. I got nowhere. I was way too antsy to read, so I went out to the living room. Dad had his laptop open and was holding the phone, drumming his fingers on the desk, scowling.

"Dad," I said. "There's strange stuff going on. Stuff I can't understand."

He looked up. "None of us do, Lucas. Women are tough. I'm the first to admit it."

"That's not what I mean," I said. "Dad, did you ever hear of something called the Annoyance Bureau?"

"No," he said, "but if there were one, you can believe I'd be calling them right now. I've been waiting all day for this e-mail from Hong Kong, and now I've lost my Internet connection. I've been trying to call the stupid help line. Listen to this." He pressed speakerphone.

". . . are busy assisting other customers," I heard one of those sugary voice-mail recordings say. "Calls will be answered in the order in which they were received. Please stay on the line. You will not be disconnected."

Click. We were disconnected.

"See what I mean? This is maddening!" He dialed again. "So, what's that you were starting to tell me?" He put the speakerphone on again.

"Your call is important to us. Please stay on the line. Your call will be answered in approximately"—the voice changed to a digitized computer voice—"four hundred eighty-three"—and back to sugary again—"minutes."

Click. We were disconnected.

"No!" Dad shook his head. "I'm sorry. This is unaccept-able. I'm calling the president of the company. Soon as I get to work tomorrow, I'm going to get his number—"

The phone rang. Dad was rummaging for a pen. "You mind picking that up for me, Lucas?"

"Hello?" I said.

"We apologize for any difficulty you have been experienc-ing," said the sugary voice.

Since when did help line recordings call you back?

"We regret any annoyance it may have caused you. Your service will be restored in approximately—"

Bzzzzzzzzzt! It was the gizmo! Then Izzy's voice came on the line. "How's thirty seconds sound to you? So, Lucas, how you feeling? You covered a lot of ground today, my friend."

Then the syrupy voice-mail recording was back. "Please try your e-mail again. This recording will not be repeated."

"Dad!" I said. "Dad! Try your e-mail."

I held my breath.

"Well, well, well," Dad said as the NEW MAIL HAS ARRIVED. WOULD YOU LIKE TO READ IT NOW? message appeared on the screen. "Who'd have believed it? To what do we owe this miracle?"

"Izzy?" I said into the phone.

"Is he what?" Dad said. "Lucas, who are you talking to?"

I put my finger to my lips. "Hello?" I said again. "Yeah. I'm here."

"I know that," Izzy said. "That was never in doubt. Inspect, detect, protect, correct, remember? So, you ready for lesson two?"

CHAPTER 8

"*So, what exactly would an apprentice do?*" I asked Izzy on Monday morning. I still wasn't sure about this, but I'd headed for Book World as soon as Dad and Claire left for work. I'd found him in the same spot as yesterday, on the top floor by the escalator.

"He keeps his eyes and ears open," he said. "Misses nothing. Is alert to annoyances big and small—"

"That's what I do all the time," I said.

He raised his index finger in the air. "My point precisely."

"There's only one thing," I said. "I've got to be outside in, like, forty minutes. I've got to . . ." Gladys was taking me to Trims for Tykes. Then I was meeting her at the pediatrician's office because Calvin needed a shot. Telling Izzy this seemed almost as bad as having to do it.

"I'll give you the whirlwind annoyance tour, then. Walk with me to the self-improvement section. Always fertile ground."

We'd barely gotten out of Gardening when Hildegund stalked over to us. "Agent Gribitz!" she said. "Did you turn in your forms?"

"What are you doing here?" Izzy said. "I don't recall inviting you into my territory."

She stepped closer. Hildegund was a head taller than Izzy even without her hat. She outweighed him by fifty pounds. I was almost sure I saw her checking out my hair. "We haven't seen a single report from you, Agent," she said. "Not your last week's progress report, or your monthly goals for this month or last month, or your weekly action plan, or your personal self-assessment. And it's not as if you just learned about them. You've had two full months. You've gotten regular reminders in your in-box." She puffed out her chest, tucked in her chin, raised her eyebrows, and peered down her nose, which was long. "I presume you know when the year-end report is due?"

"Let me see. Would that be year-end?" he said.

She was right up in his face now. "We are not on a calendar-year basis, Agent Gribitz. Our fiscal year ends on the first Tuesday before the last Friday of the last month. Which in this case is Christmas Eve. In other words, tomorrow night."

He didn't move. "And who died and made you the paperwork police?"

"The Higher-ups. Of which I am one. Which you would know if you read your bureau bulletins. We've got our eye on you, Agent Gribitz. We're watching your every move. Let me remind you: There's a job open in the Lapland office, so if those reports aren't in on time, and I mean every single one—"

"Been there, done that." He waved his hand. "Lapland, Tibet, the Kalahari. And let *me* remind *you* that I left them all less annoying than I found them, and that in each instance the Higher-ups there begged me to come back."

"That was then. This is now," she said. "So unless you want to spend Christmas with a bunch of reindeer, I'd get my ducks in line, do some serious prioritizing, make sure my action plan was—"

"My action plan, madam, is not to waste time filling out reports. My short-term plan is to keep the annoyance level in my territory at a reasonable level. Call me a dreamer, but my long-term plan is to do the same for New York City. My immediate goal is to rid myself of pedunculated pissants!"

Bzzzzzzzt! The gizmo went off.

"Sorry, dollface. Duty calls. Gotta hop." He gave her a pat, looked over at me, winked, and pressed a button.

BEEP-bee-BEEP-bee-BEE-BEEEE! Beep-bee-BEEP-bee-BEEEEEEE!

She began hopping around like her feet were on fire.

"Stop that at once! Turn that thing off!" she squealed, still jumping.

"Let's go, Lucas." He took my arm. "Nice moves, poop-sie!" he called to her. "And by the way, that's herd of reindeer, not bunch."

"I'm warning you," she screamed. "It's dark and cold in Lapland at this time of year!"

"Is that 'Sweetly Sings the Donkey'?" I asked as we hurried down the aisle. "Or 'The Itsy Bitsy Spider'?"

"I'd go with 'Donkey,'" he said.

"Izzy, what's a pedunculated pissant?" I was laughing.

"One cut above a crapulent carbuncle. Adieu, O crapulent carbuncle!" he called over his shoulder. "By the way, Lucas, if you're going to be my apprentice, you need to stop calling it a gizmo." He stopped walking. "This, my friend, is the annoyometron. Burned-out bureaucrats may use walkie-talkies. Those of us more technologically advanced—"

"Annoyometron? That sounds like a Transformer. It's an annoyometron?"

"*Absolutamente.* Invented and named by yours truly." He

bowed. "You realize, of course, that I used to be a Higher-up. High up in the Higher-ups. But, as I started to say, a clever agent has many means at his disposal. Not just techno-logical—oho!" His index finger went up. "Speaking of disposal, I just had a brilliant idea for a Lucas demo." He checked his watch. "It'll just take an instant." He led me to the far wall and over to a door.

Maybe the annoyometron would pop open like the nuts, transform to vehicle mode, turn into a robot. . . .

He must have guessed what I was thinking. "No, Lucas," he said. "This is the closet. Where the Santa suit lives. I'd been thinking it was just as well you have to leave, since my dreaded Santa duty looms. . . ."

Sure enough, there was the Santa Claus suit on a hanger. "But now . . ." He snapped his fingers. It disappeared—beard, pillow, and all.

"It vanished!" I said. "Like the smells! Then, the Annoy-ance Bureau doesn't only deal with small stuff! And the annoyometron did that?"

"No," he said. "I did it. And alas, it's not really gone. Only redistributed, to some Santa-suit-deprived place. It will return, but if I'm lucky, not till after Christmas, which means"—he waggled his eyebrows—"that due to circum-stances entirely outside my control, I will be unable to waste precious time on that intensely infuriating, utterly useless Santa gig, and instead can use our considerable resources and talents doing more constructive and entertaining things—"

"Like what?" Maybe now was when he turned into a robot.

Bzzzzzzzzzt!

He looked at the gizmo and hurried down the aisle to the escalators. I ran after him. He leaned over the railing. From here we could see both the main floor and the balcony. "Oh, no," he sighed. "Lucas, look at that!" He pointed to a kid about my age standing on the balcony level whose jacket sleeve was stuck to his mouth.

"Whoa! He's Velcroed his cuff to his braces," I said as the kid struggled to pull his sleeve free before anyone noticed. I could see myself doing that.

"Small stuff to us. Big stuff to him. We'll help him out," Izzy said. "Observe closely!"

The jacket dropped off the boy's braces onto the floor. He looked baffled but happy.

"And was that the annoyometron?"

"No, that time I used simple Annoyance Bureau powers. Some might call it extranatural, if you get my drift." He checked the annoyometron again and glanced once more at his watch. "So, Lucas, to review," he said as we took the escalator to the first floor and walked to the café, which was in the back and up three stairs. "Sometimes we use technology . . . wait a minute! Wait a minute!"

He pointed to a very big man sitting with a little boy. The boy was spooning up tiny bites of a brownie with chocolate ice cream and whipped cream. You could tell he was trying to make it last. The man stared at the brownie. He leaned closer and closer. He picked up a huge spoon. I could almost see his tongue hanging out as he reached for the boy's plate. "Gonna eat that?" I heard him say.

"Do something!" I told Izzy.

"Okay. As I was saying, sometimes we use technology. Sometimes we go extranatural. And sometimes"—he pulled something from his pocket—"all you need is a . . ."

Green plastic water pistol? Not an ionic displacer rifle? Not a photon cannon?

But I couldn't help laughing as the man yelled, "Hey!"

and dropped his spoon and jumped up, wiping water from his face. I almost didn't hear Izzy talking to me as we ran down the café stairs and over to an empty table.

"So, what do you think, Lucas? This line of work appeal to you? You feel like taking on this so-called small stuff?"

Before I could answer, he'd reached in his coat pocket and pulled out a pencil and pad. "Here's something to get you started. Draw a line down the center of the page. On the left side write, 'I hate it when, dot, dot, dot.' On the other side put, 'You know what drives me up the wall?' It can be things, words, actions, anything that annoys you, irks you, irritates you . . ."

I looked at him. "You're asking me to make a list?"

"And why not?"

"I don't know. I thought I might get an annoyometron. I thought"—I felt ridiculous saying it—"you were going to give me a mission. I thought"—now I really felt ridiculous—"you might make me vanish."

"Why would you want to vanish?" he said. "We're just getting started."

Because I was supposed to be meeting Gladys in five minutes to go to Trims for Tykes. . . .

"We're not on Cybertron, my friend," he said. "This is planet Earth. New York City. Book World. And this is the Annoyance Bureau. It may seem as if we deal in the small stuff. But to the person who's annoyed, there is no small stuff. When you can't fix it, it's never small. And it's always personal. Remember that. And make no mistake: You have a mission."

CHAPTER 9

The average age at Trims for Tykes was five. The barber chairs were merry-go-round horsies. The music was Alvin and the Chipmunks.

"Calvin!" Gladys leaned across me and whispered. "What's Lukey writing?"

"Nothing." I covered the pad with my arm. Izzy'd said I should put down everything I thought of. I had more than a page already.

- water up your nose
- crumbs in the bed
- the Microsoft talking paper clip
- unscratchable itches
- slimy egg whites
- canned green beans
- phone numbers that are all letters
- busy signals
- snoring
- car commercials
- telemarketers
- when all the paper falls out of your binder

- when the filling of your taco falls out on your foot
- those perfumed cards that fall out of magazines
- jingle-bell earrings
- squeaking shoes
- barbers in Santa hats
- people who look over your shoulder while you're writing
- being called Lukey!!!!
- people who address their questions about you to someone else instead of asking you

"I think he's writing to Santa, Calvin!" Gladys whispered.

- whispering

"Should we tell him he's a little late? It's only two more days to Christmas!"

- Erasers that don't work

I could keep doing this forever. Except that someone was standing over me. I shoved the list inside a copy of *Big Backyard* and pretended to be deeply engrossed in connecting the dots without a crayon.

"Okay, young man," he said. "You're next."

Could it be? My heart started beating really fast. I didn't dare look up.

Calvin began to bark.

"Woof, woof yourself, Bowser!"

It was Izzy, in a white barber coat. I jumped up.

"Follow me, young man. That's right," he said. "Straight back. We have a special salon for our more mature customers."

Gladys started after us.

"Not you, madam." He held up his hand. "You wait here."

"Okay!" she said. "As long as you give him a good shaping! We're going to see Dr. Scotty now, aren't we, Calvin? Lukey, you remember how to get to Dr. Scotty's office?"

"Yes." She'd told me twenty times.

"Now, make sure you take enough off!" she told Izzy, grabbing hold of both sides of my head and holding my hair straight out. Every barber, mom, and baby-sitter in the place was watching. "Bushy is for bushes, isn't that right, Calvin! Not for big, handsome boys—"

"Say no more, madam!" Izzy said. "He's in good hands. You ready for a good shaping, young man?" He hustled me past the kids on horses getting their haircuts and, calling, "Toodle-oo, sweet pea!" led me through a door to a back room.

"How'd you find me?" I said.

"I can't believe my own apprentice is asking me that question." He checked the annoyometron. "Good thing I remembered to turn off the beep. She'd have blown the fuse! I already told you: An annoyance professional inspects, detects, protects, and corrects. The Correct function doesn't always work as well as I'd hope. Detect, however, works perfectly"—he nodded at his barber coat—"and the bureau's costume room also came in handy."

He led me out a door, through another room, down a hallway, and past a row of trash cans to some stairs. We'd gone down two flights when I noticed a strong sauerkraut smell. Two more flights, through another door, and I was free! We were in a dingy passage that smelled like school lunch. "Now what?" I asked Izzy as we started walking.

"Depends how much time we have. How long does a haircut take?"

"I don't know," I said. "I avoid them whenever possible."

"So, half an hour? With that mop on you, maybe an hour."

There were carts coming toward us. "Where does this go?" I asked. Trims for Tykes was all the way across town from Book World.

"Anywhere you want," he said.

A man wearing the same reflector shades as the guys yesterday walked by pushing a hand truck piled with rolling backpacks.

"Distribution!" I said. "Redistribution! They're moving annoying things around!"

Izzy nodded. "Bingo!"

More carts went by, one with oversize umbrellas, another with smiley-face pins, another with big fat purple candles that smelled like grape jelly. I saw cartons of Tofu Pups, kids' drum sets, many Barbies, crates of cigars, spitballs, mothballs, meatballs, and even—I was almost sure—hair balls.

"Catch ya later," the Annoyance Bureau guys all called to Izzy as they trudged past. "See you at the meeting."

Izzy kept shaking his head. "Thousands of operatives moving thousands of annoyances, and it's still not enough."

"So who decides what stays, what goes, and what goes where?" I said. I loved meatballs.

"Who else? The Higher-ups. A committee of Higher-ups. Higher-ups too high up to have any idea what's going on in the field. Higher-ups who wouldn't know a . . . you sure you want to get me started?"

"Where are they taking this stuff?"

"Some of it"—he pointed to a wheelbarrow full of Pokémon cards—"goes directly to new venues. 'Venues'? Phagh!" He made a face. "I hope you're keeping an annoying-word list! Some goes to distribution centers. This guy"—he nodded toward a large scarecrow bungee-corded to a hand truck, squawking a recorded announcement about farm-fresh vegetables—"is headed for the Repository." He pointed to an unmarked metal door up ahead. "The final resting place. For the worst of the worst."

As we got close I heard loud beeps and bleeps and robotic voices: "Welcome! You've got mail!" "Please stand clear of the moving platform!" "Please hang up!" "Please stay on the line!" "Please remember to take your belongings!" "The options have changed. Please listen closely to the new menu!" "Your connection has been lost!"

"Great! Terrific!" Izzy snorted. "One of these turkeys must have left a drawer open."

"I thought you said it was the final resting place," I said. "I hear this stuff all the time."

"Yes, well"—he shook his finger—"once again the Higher-ups, in their infinite wisdom . . . as I said yesterday, the difference between what should be and what is . . . you hungry?"

I nodded.

We walked a little farther. He opened a door. We went up many stairs and through another door into a crowded coffee shop. The stools were patched with duct tape. The tinsel hanging from the ceiling looked like it had been there since 1902.

"Two ostrich burgers, please, Mabel," he told the waitress as we sat down in the only empty booth.

"Same for you folks?" I heard her ask the people in the booth next to us—agents, by their green coats and the walkie-talkies on the table. Everyone except the waitress was dressed like an agent. "Ostrich special and prune juice all around? What about you, sir? The same?"

"Yeah, and a cauliflower cheese. And make it snappy. We've got a meeting to go to."

Mabel brought us each a tiny glass of bluish green radioactive-looking juice. "On the house," she said.

"Don't touch it, Lucas!" Izzy warned. "It's wheat grass juice. It's horrible. Why hasn't this been confiscated?" he asked Mabel. "I marked it for the Repository last week!" The annoyometron had started beeping when she brought the juice. It was still beeping. "And what about that?" He pointed at a strip of flypaper, loaded with shriveled flies, dangling from the ceiling. "And that oatmeal's been here since the Fourth of July! And Christmas decorations on a begonia? I know this isn't my territory, but is anyone in charge here?"

The annoyometron was still beeping. "Shut that infernal thing off!" an agent yelled.

"Turn it off, Izzy," Mabel said. "And be careful what you say. The walls have ears."

"The walls have cockroaches!" he shouted, flicking one off. "Have all you agents gone numb? Or are you asleep at the switch? Who's policing the annoyance police?" He shook his head. "I've said it before, Lucas: If I were a different sort of guy, I'd be taking this personally."

"You're gonna drive yourself crazy, Izzy," Mabel said as she removed the blue juice. "It's not worth it."

"Not worth it?" he said. "If it's not worth it, I might as well give up. What do you think, Lucas?"

"I can see why you're annoyed," I said.

"See that, Mabel?" He reached over and gave me a pat. "Lucas gets it."

She'd brought our ostrich burgers. I opened the bun in case there were feathers sticking out, or chunks of beak. The two of them were watching me, waiting for me to eat. I drowned it in ketchup and took a tiny bite. "How is it?" they both said.

"Not that bad." Mom and Dad would be proud of me.

"Not that bad?" Izzy exclaimed. "It's delicious! And would you believe the Higher-ups issued a removal order? Luckily, yours truly intercepted it. Now they're the house specialty."

I took a bigger bite. It was good.

"Mabel's an agent, right?" I asked when she'd walked away. "That's why she can hear you?"

"That's one reason," he said. "But anyone can hear me if I haven't pressed the Mute function."

"On the gizmo?"

"Certainly on the gizmo. What? You thought this was magic or something? This isn't the Middle Ages, Lucas. We're talking science, here."

"I see." I didn't. "And it's seriously called an annoyometron?"

"Why? You got a problem with that?" He put down his burger. "You got a better name?"

"No, it just sounds so much like a Transformer name. You know"—I thought back to some of my old Transformer toys—"Galvatron, Computron, Megatron . . . what else does it do?"

"Whatever I tell it to," he said. "Inspects, detects, protects, and corrects. Usually. Sometimes."

"Can it make things spin?"

His eyebrows went up. "Spin? Not that I know of. It does occasionally make things hop."

"Uh"—my eyebrows went up too—"I know."

"What, you think I'm a terrible guy for doing that to her?"

"No, I thought it was funny."

"It's not funny! That woman hates me like poison, Lucas. Hildegund's had it in for me ever since I confiscated her last name."

I stopped chewing. "What?"

"You heard me. I expunged it not only from the record, but out of existence. Sent it to the Repository, where I trust it remains, safely under lock and key."

"What was her name?"

He rolled his eyes. "Grabitz! The entire world thought we were related. Or, heaven forfend, married!"

When I stopped laughing, I told him about Tinkerbell, which made him laugh till he choked and his water came out his nose, which made me laugh harder. This ostrich burger was growing on me. I was sorry to see the end of it.

"Another round?" he asked, wiping his eyes.

"Yeah. Sure!"

He signaled to Mabel. She came over and nodded toward the other agents, who were getting ready to go. She frowned when he gave her the order. "Izzy, you don't have time!"

"Let me worry about that," he said. "Okay, Lucas. Back to the name. We need something that conveys its purpose. And the full range of its powers. Some of which, like this Spin function of yours, seem to take us in directions unknown and highly promising."

"Hopomatic?" I suggested. "Spinomatic? No. Too much like a washing machine."

"You do know that it measures annoyance levels," he said.

"How 'bout annoyometer?" I said.

Mabel came back with two more plates. I saw her frowning at the gizmo. "I wouldn't be flashing that around, Izzy," she said. "It's not wise."

"I'm a big boy, Mabel," he said. "I know what I'm doing. It also corrects levels, Lucas. I'm speaking ideally here, of course. We still have a few kinks to iron out—"

"Izzy, please. You don't want trouble." Mabel was looking more and more worried.

"Mabel's the only reason I bother with this dive," he told me when she'd left. "Mabel and the ostrich burgers. Annoyotron?" he said through a humongous mouthful.

"That sounds too big," I said. This burger was even better than the last one. "It's only six inches long. Annoyotron junior?"

"No way! Vexometer? That's got a nicely annoying ring."

"Definitely not. Vexostat?"

"Forget it!"

"I have it!" I said. "This is a really annoying name. Irkostat."

"Lucas"—his face lit up—"if I had a gold star, I'd put it on your forehead! Irkostat! Speaking of heads"—he eyed my hair—"what is your family's problem? They want you to have limp, wimpy hair, hair that lies there like a doormat?"

"I'm fairly sure they do," I said.

"Listen to me." He raised his index finger. "Hair springs forth from the head, which houses the brain, which in your case is a veritable . . . let's just say the hair is an expression of the spirit beneath."

"Really?" I checked myself in the mirrored tiles. My hair was more like a large porcupine than a doormat. "And that's good?"

"*Absolutamente*. So, what's the story? Are we cutting it?"

"Not if I can help it," I said.

"Lucas"—he leaned toward me—"you can help it."

"Okay." I took a deep breath. "Then, no."

"It's settled, then. A stand-up guy with stand-up hair. No haircut for Lucas. And if your horrifying friend Gladys has issues . . . 'issues'! Add that to your list."

"Okay." I'd already thought of *Gladys, squeegee, mucilage, Elpidio.*

The agents had suddenly gotten up and were filing by our table.

"Eat up there, Gribitz!" one said. "You don't want to be late. Not today."

"Enforcement's around," said another. "Word to the wise, Gribby boy. Lose the device!"

"Chop-chop, Gribitz. You show up late again, the Big Cheese is gonna have a cow!"

"What are you doing, Izzy?" Mabel said. "Come on. Please! Let's go."

I jumped up, but Izzy sat there chewing.

"Come on!" I said. "Izzy, you're gonna get in trouble."

I looked at my watch. He wasn't the only one. I was supposed to have met Gladys an hour ago.

CHAPTER
10

Mabel and the cook were gone. Izzy was still eating.

"How could I have forgotten?" I asked him.

"You forgot because you were having a nice time," he said. "You'll take the passages, as you call them. It'll get you from anywhere to everywhere. If you don't get lost, and you know the right door, it's never far." He'd already explained the system of signposts and address markers, which involved numbers and letters etched into the walls. It sounded complicated. "They parallel the streets and avenues overhead, with the occasional zig or zag. They run below the sewers and below the subway tunnels. There should be a map, but big surprise, there isn't. Nor are there bathroom facilities or food or water. Though you can find food, if you don't mind helping yourself from the carts. Don't worry. You won't get lost. You're smart."

He wiped his mouth. And finally stood up. And finally headed for the stairs. "More than smart. As witness the name irkostat! And discovering the Spin function."

"You think I should hold on to the irkostat for you?" I said as we went down the stairs. I was getting more and more nervous. About both of us. "It might be wise."

"That's another word for your list, Lucas! 'Wise.' You're an even bigger worrywart than Mabel. And thanks, but no thanks. An Annoyance Bureau meeting at HQ with the Higher-ups? No, no. This baby stays with me!"

"So, you think you got that?" he said once we were in the passages and he'd explained the signpost system one more time.

I repeated the instructions to him.

"I'll tell you what I tell myself," he said. "The best defense is a good offense. The customer is always wrong. Wish me luck at the meeting, kiddo. This was great. I can't remember when I've had such a good time."

"Me too," I called as he turned and headed off. "Wish me luck too."

Listen, Gladys—I practiced as I ran down the passage—*there's nothing wrong with my hair. I like my hair. My hair is this way because it's the way I want it. It's an expression of my spirit. I'm a stand-up guy with stand-up hair. And even if I had wanted a haircut, which I don't . . .*

Carts and hand trucks were going by. I was too busy keeping track of my turns and watching out for street and building markers to notice what was in them, too busy with my Gladys speech. Until I noticed a wheelbarrow full of hats—large purple straw hats, umbrella hats, pinwheel hats, puffy Rasta hats, and lots of those multicolored South American knitted thingies with the tassel hanging from the point and earflaps that tied under the chin.

I stopped running. "Sir. Excuse me, sir. Are those your hats?"

"Nope," he said. "I'm just moving 'em from here to there."

"Well, d'you think the bureau would mind if . . ."

I thought he'd be mad that I knew about the bureau, but he said, "Not if they don't know. A few hats more or less . . ."

A few hats! That was it! I could get a hat for Calvin, too. Say it was a Christmas present. I could get one for Gladys. That way it wouldn't look weird when they saw me wearing one. It would explain why I was so late. Izzy was right. I was smart.

I picked two big ones and a little one, put one on, tucked all my hair inside, and tied the earflaps under my chin.

"Oh, it's you, pal! Most definitely." The guy nodded. "Orange is your color."

I reached in my pocket. "How much?"

"Nothin'," he said. "Merry Christmas from the bureau. They itch."

"Thanks!" I couldn't worry about that. I had to find my way out of there.

Left. Right. Another right. The passage smelled like tuna fish, then hair spray, then goats. I ran till I found the marker Izzy'd told me to watch for, opened the next door, took the steps two at a time, and came out in the lobby of a fancy building.

My head was sweating. The hat did itch. Good thing I didn't take it off, though, because when I looked out the big, fancy double doors, I saw Gladys pacing back and forth, peering up and down the sidewalk. Miss Piggy meets Godzilla.

"Do you know how long we've been waiting?" she screamed when she saw me. Calvin was crying. I couldn't tell if it was the shot or Gladys. "Where were you?"

I knew what Izzy would have said: *Right in here, toots. Where were you?* But I'd only been his apprentice since yesterday. "Sorry," I said. "I'm really sorry." She hadn't asked how I'd gotten inside without her seeing me. I prayed she wouldn't think of it.

"Do you know how cold it is standing out here?" She pointed to a sign on top of a building. "Fourteen degrees! Without the windchill! Not that you'd know, out gallivanting. I was worried sick, and this poor baby's been crying for the last hour!"

"Sorry," I said again. Calvin looked so pathetic. He was slumped inside one of those sleeping-bag things. His nose was running. He had tears frozen on his face. I hated shots too. I could remember every shot I ever had. I squatted down by the stroller and reached in my backpack. "Look at this, Calvin. Look, I brought you something. Something very cool." I held out the little hat, then pointed to my head. "See," I said, "brother hats."

He stopped crying.

"You want to wear it, Calvin?"

His eyes brightened. He sat up straighter. "Woof!"

I took off the hat he was wearing, put the new one on him, and tied the earflaps under his chin. "You look extremely cool," I said.

He smiled and woofed.

"That's my good boy!" Gladys said to him. She turned to me. "That was very thoughtful of you, dearie."

Whew! I stood up and handed her the other hat. "Uh, this one's for you."

"You didn't have to do that!" She held it out like it might bite, but she seemed pleased. "What do you call this type of hat? It's so quaint! Wherever did you find it?"

It was good a cab came along then. It was even better Calvin barked the whole way home, because I could pretend I didn't hear when Gladys asked how my haircut went. Now I just had to decide whether to let Claire see I hadn't cut my hair. Plan B being to keep the hat on till I went home to Connecticut.

✻ ✻ ✻

"Lucas, why are you wearing your hat in the house?"

Phoebe came in my room the minute we got home. She had three friends with her today, Zoë, Chloe, and a Zoë/Chloe clone.

I stuffed my lists in the drawer. "I like to. My head is cold."

"How could your head be cold?" she said. "It's boiling in here." She had on a tank top. They all did. "Come on!" She sat down on my bed and tucked her legs under her. "Take it off. We want to see your haircut."

"There's nothing to see," I said.

"Yes, there is. You went to"—she made quote marks in the air—"Trims for Tykes." She looked at her friends. "We want to see. Right?"

"No," I said.

"Why not? Because you look like a dork?"

"No."

"Come on, Lucas. It has to be better than before." She rolled her eyes. "We need to see."

"Maybe later." I went into the bathroom. Too bad I hadn't brought the lists in with me. *Dork* was definitely going on it. Along with everything else Phoebe said and did.

"And why won't he take the hat off?" I heard through the door. "This is getting interesting. See, Chloe, I told you he had a girlfriend. This hat is his Christmas present from *her.* That's why he won't take it off. What's her name, Lucas? You can tell us."

"There's no girlfriend," I called. "It's just . . . I've bonded with this hat."

That was a thought. Maybe I should glue it on.

The instant I came out of the bathroom, she snatched it off my head.

77

Her hands went to her mouth. "Look at him. He didn't cut his hair. Sneaky, Lucas. Very sneaky."

"Are you gonna tell Claire?"

That was the exact wrong thing for me to say.

A sly and fiendish look came over her. More sly and fiendish, even, than her usual look. "I don't know." She threw the hat to Zoë. Or Chloe, who threw it to Schmoe, who threw it back to Phoebe. "What's it worth to you?"

"Nothing." I hated how my voice sounded. "Go ahead and tell Claire. See if I care." I tried to grab the hat from her.

She scooted away. "Liar." She opened the window. "Let's see if those earflaps can flap like a bird." She held the hat out the window. "Fly away, little hat. Flap, flap! Or maybe I'll wear it." She put it on and started dancing around. Her friends broke out laughing. "I could actually use a new hat." She went over, looked at herself in the mirror, and made a face. "Or maybe not." She pulled it off. "Eeooh. Hat head." She fluffed up her hair. "What'll you give me if I don't tell my mom about your hair?"

"Anything you want."

Was this really me saying that? It was a good thing Izzy hadn't heard it.

"Hmm. Let's see." She tipped her head to one side and put her hands on her hips. "Let me think. There is that book report. You've read *The Last of the Mohicans*, haven't you, Lucas? There's also my paper on the scientific method. Wow. There are so many possibilities. . . ."

If there was ever a moment for Izzy to appear, this was it. But Izzy'd already rescued me once today. And Izzy had his own problems.

CHAPTER 11

Phoebe did give the hat back finally. I didn't bother putting it on. She'd blab to Claire no matter what I did for her or how much she promised.

Calvin refused to take his hat off. He even had his nap wearing it. He was still wearing it when Dad and Claire got home.

"Calvin! Great hat! Where'd you get it?" Dad said after they'd each picked him up and kissed him hello.

"Aren't you too hot wearing it in the house?" Claire said. "Wouldn't you like to take it off now?" She tried to untie the earflaps.

"Grrrrrrrrrr!" he growled at her.

"It's from me," I said. "He loves it. And we've been reading." He'd come into my room after his nap while I was working on my annoying-things list.

- static electricity
- nosebleeds
- prank calls
- warts
- bickering

- paper cuts
- toenail clippings

Calvin had brought in *The Little Engine That Could.* We'd read it nine or ten times.

"This is so sweet of you, Lucas," Claire was saying. "Where'd you buy it?"

I was about to say "On the street," which was true—sort of—when Phoebe came in. "Lucas?" She pretended to be puzzled. "Weren't you getting a haircut this morning?"

Dad and Claire both looked at me like, *Oh. That's right.*

Time for my stand-up guy speech. "I thought I was too. But then . . ."

"Ye-e-e-e-s?" Phoebe's eyebrow went up. She wasn't just a bully. She was a sneaky bully.

"I went to the place and . . . this guy comes up to me and says to follow him to the back. So I followed him. I mean, he was wearing the white barber coat and everything. Gladys can tell you. But it turned out he wasn't a barber."

I felt like I'd stepped off a cliff.

"What do you mean, he wasn't a barber?" Dad was frowning. "What was he, then? And why didn't someone else take care of you?"

"Well, uh . . . "

I'd stepped off a cliff and was hanging in midair.

"Trims for Tykes is the best children's hair salon in the city." Claire looked confused. "How could he not be a barber? How could you tell?"

"Oh, I could tell," I said. "Believe me."

I could see they didn't.

I tried Izzy's line: "You sure you want to get me started?"

They clearly did.

"So, then, you're . . . saying he was a barber impersonator." Dad had his lawyer face on. "This is a very odd story, Lucas."

"He wasn't a barber impersonator exactly. He was more like . . . " Was it worse if I made Izzy sound insane, or me? "A barber wannabe. It was sad, actually. I felt sort of sorry for him. I mean, this guy didn't even have real scissors."

Gladys came in from the kitchen. "I could have told you there was something off there! I didn't care for that barber from the start. He was very fresh with me."

"He was nice to me," I said. "I just didn't think it was that good an idea letting him cut my hair." I looked at Claire. "Not with Christmas coming up and all."

"So then what happened?" Phoebe said. I'd been hoping that if I didn't look at her she'd get bored and go away.

"Uh . . . a real barber came in and told him to leave. And so he did. And so then I asked the real barber if he could cut my hair, but he said, 'Forget it!' He said they were, like, totally booked. Overbooked, in fact. In fact, all the way till New Year's."

That last touch was probably what killed me.

Phoebe's eyebrow was all the way up to her scalp.

Claire was looking at Dad like, *He's your son, Charles. You deal with it.*

"Lucas"—Dad shook his head—"if I didn't know you better, I'd say that story was fishier than our dinner."

"So now what do we do about this hair?" Claire said.

"We'll figure that out tomorrow," Dad said. "Let's get this meal under way. Because if you all still want to go out shopping . . ." I threw him a quick thank-you look. He raised his eyebrow. "Lucas, Phoebe"—he nodded toward the dining room—"set the table."

"If you're going to lie, Lucas," Phoebe said as soon as they were in the kitchen, "at least make it a good one. That was without a doubt the lamest—"

"Ask Gladys!" I said. "You heard her say the guy looked weird. Go on. Ask her."

Gladys was staying to baby-sit while we went out.

"Oh. Don't worry. I will." She got the napkins and chopsticks from the drawer. "And how long are you staying here?"

"Till Sunday," I said.

"*The Last of the Mohicans* is about eight thousand pages. Better start reading."

"What are you talking about?" I said. "The deal's off!"

"No, it's not," she said. "I didn't tell her, did I?"

"You couldn't," I said. "She saw my hair." I'd have to add *not-too-bright bullies* to my list.

"Some people like *The Last of the Mohicans*," she said, refolding the napkin I'd just folded. "And I hope you like raw fish."

"I wanted to get us something special," Claire told me once all of us, including Gladys, were at the table. "*Negihama, hamachi,* giant clam, eel rolls"—she pointed out each of the fish items—"and *ikura* for Calvin. Calvin loves sushi. Right, Calvin?" Calvin bounced up and down in his high chair like he could hardly wait. "We all do. Lucas, you know, when I first met your dad, he wouldn't even eat *fried* fish. Now he could eat sushi twice a day."

I looked at the platter of pale, pinkish, flabby slabs of fish laid out on blobs of cold rice. Except for the *ikura*, which was little orange balls on top of rice blobs wrapped in seaweed. I didn't *want* to be afraid of dinner. . . .

"Those are raw fish eggs, in case you're wondering," Phoebe whispered.

Had I already listed *whispering?*

"Help yourself, sweetie," Claire told me. "They're really good."

Calvin was picking fish eggs off his rice one at a time. Everyone else was scarfing down whole pieces of sushi, going, "Oh, yum! Mmmm! This is so good!" Only Gladys was sitting there like, *I'll have peanut butter, if you don't mind.*

"I keep telling Gladys she needs to get with the program," Dad teased her.

"That's why I picked up some asparagus rolls for her," Claire said.

Asparagus two nights in a row? This couldn't be happening. And now she was looking at me. "Try one, Lucas."

Where was Tinkerbell when I needed him?

"The eel is cooked," Dad said.

I put an eel roll in my mouth and followed it with a gigantic slug of milk.

Not a good combo.

Phoebe saw me start to gag. She also saw me take something that looked like a wet eraser off a blob of rice, eat the rice, and slip the eraser in my pocket. But she kept quiet till there were several slabs of fish and several asparagus chunks in my pocket. Then she leaned toward me and whispered, "I'd be thinking about the scientific method if I were you."

I was thinking about Izzy. I couldn't wait to hear what he'd say about my afternoon. And about my lists, which were growing by the minute. "Dad, can we go to Book World after dinner?" I said.

"Good idea," he said. So after we'd cleaned up and I'd emptied my pocket into the toilet, and we'd worked out that we'd drop Phoebe at Colossus Records and pick her up when we were done, Dad, Claire, Phoebe, and I went out.

Claire had spent most of dinner discussing Christmas—

holly or pine boughs for the apartment, or both? What kind of cookies to bake tomorrow? What wine with dinner? Claire was psyched. The Christmas prep talk continued after we left. I listened only enough to make sure the word *hair* didn't come up. I'd brought my annoyance lists to show Izzy. I kept finding things to add.

- galoshes on dogs
- seeing half a Big Bang Bacon Melt frozen in a snowdrift
- people who bash you with their shopping bags and say, "Watch where you're going!"
- people who say, "Have a good one!"

Izzy would love that, especially because it was the agents outside Book World saying it.

I looked for him as soon as we got inside. I saw Pellet and company bustling around with clipboards and walkie-talkies. I saw grouchy shoppers, irritated cashiers, disgusted security guards, and exhausted salesclerks. Book World was like Annoyance Central. So where was he? Why didn't I hear any beeps or buzzes? And why was the *Howl-iday Pet Treat* book back—a whole display of them? I saw all sorts of things Izzy would never stand for: calendars of dogs in bonnets, racks of books two inches tall for $12.95, a zillion Barney items. I tried telling myself they'd always been there, that I was just noticing them more now that I was Izzy's apprentice. But I was getting a bad feeling.

"I'm going to look for some gifts, if that's okay," I told Dad. "I'll meet you by the escalator in ten minutes."

The agents were in the self-improvement section. I started over to them.

"No respect for procedure whatsoever!" I heard Agent Zapp say. "And definitely not a people person."

"I've said that for years!" Agent Tuber nodded. "I saw this coming a mile away."

Agent Pellet was nodding too. "I don't know why they let it go on so long! You can't have a loose cannon like that interfacing with the public."

I could picture Izzy if he had heard them say he "interfaced." Because they were talking about him. I was sure of it. I stepped closer.

"I know, but couldn't they just have given him a cart, put him on the Staten Island run?" Agent Bramble was saying.

Agent Zapp shook his head. "Pandora, you're too much of a softy."

My bad feeling was getting worse.

I cleared my throat. They stopped talking. "Uh, I'm sorry to bother you," I said. "Do you by any chance know where—"

They turned their heads away.

"Excuse me." I walked up to Agent Pellet, who'd begun unloading a whole stack of *Overcoming the Annoying Habits*. "Why are you putting those books back? Is something up with Izzy?"

"Oh, something's up, all right," said Agent Zapp.

The look he gave me sent chills down my spine.

Hildegund was behind a bookcase, writing on her clipboard. She was even larger and scarier than I remembered. I checked to make sure Claire and Dad couldn't see me. Then I went over to her. "Uh, pardon me? I'm wondering if you've seen Agent Gribitz?" My heart was racing. I prayed she didn't remember me.

She clearly did. "Agent Gribitz?" she said. "Don't you mean former agent Gribitz?"

My throat tightened. "What happened? Where'd he go? Do you know where I can find him?"

She held out a flyer. On it were two photos of Izzy, one

from the side, one full-face, looking like he was about to blow a fuse. I'd seen that expression a thousand times, but in a mug shot it made him look berserk.

WARNING! THIS INDIVIDUAL IS NO LONGER ASSOCIATED WITH ABGNY OR ANY OTHER . . .

"My guess is he's on his way to Lapland," she said.
I didn't even know where Lapland was.

"You didn't find anything?" Dad said when I met them by the escalator. His voice sound blurred and far away.
"What?"
He said it again: "You didn't find any gifts for anyone?"
"Lucas, are you all right?" Claire said.
I had to swallow a few times before I could speak. "No. Yeah. I'm okay."
"I hope it's not the sushi," I heard her say. "It's usually so reliable. Are you sick to your stomach, Lucas? Charles, he looks a little green."
"What do you say, Son?" Dad said. "Do we need to go?"
I nodded. They paid for their books. We picked Phoebe up at the record store and walked home. Calvin really wanted me to read *Little Engine* again, so I read it once for him, but then I told Claire I had a headache. At first I thought I was making that up, but it turned out I did.
Dad gave me two Tylenols. Then I went to my room. Along with the others, I'd brought a few of my old comfort books—*The Neverending Story, The Last Unicorn, Asterix and the Soothsayer*—the ones that always helped. I got in bed and tried to read. They didn't help. Izzy was gone. He'd left me.
I knew that was taking it personally, which I shouldn't do.

Which was stupid. He hadn't left me. They'd made him leave. It had nothing to do with me. I knew that.

Except that Izzy had powers. He could have gotten word to me. He could have told me he was leaving. If he'd really wanted.

CHAPTER 12

"Dad, did you get any e-mails?" I asked as soon as I got up the next morning. He and Claire had taken the day off and were at the kitchen table making shopping lists. "Is your e-mail working okay? You didn't have to call the help line for anything?" I'd thought of that during the night.

Dad looked puzzled. "My e-mail's fine. How're you feeling today? Better?"

I tried not to be disappointed, because I'd had another thought in the night too. Maybe Izzy's powers didn't belong to him. Maybe they came with the job, and when he left the bureau . . . in which case, of course he couldn't use his regular Izzy ways to get in touch with me. He'd need a phone. "Dad, do they have phones in Lapland?"

Now he really looked baffled. "Excuse me?" He turned to Claire. "If he's dreaming about Lapland, there must have been something wrong with the sushi."

I knew I shouldn't have said that. "No. I'm okay. Dad, I need to go back to Book World this morning."

Claire looked up from her shopping list. "Today's not good, Lucas. We've got so much to do." She must have seen how upset I was. "You're not worrying about buying presents for us, are you?"

I'd forgotten I hadn't bought any presents.

"It's okay," she said. "Your dad will take you out. He's going out now anyway. Charles, make sure you get a fresh turkey, not frozen. It'll never thaw in time." She listed the other things they needed. "And when you get back, Lucas, you and Phoebe can bake. And then we'll have an early dinner and go to the Christmas Eve service. You'll love it, Lucas. The music is so beautiful. It always makes me happy just to be there."

Dad and I hit every store up and down Broadway, trying to find a fresh turkey. Some of them were the stores I'd heard the agents talking about on their walkie-talkies: Food Emporium, Foodway, Food Fair, the Health Hut. I saw agents walking around in all of them. If Dad hadn't been with me, I'd have gone over and asked if they'd heard anything about Izzy.

"So, I'm relieved you've been finding enough to do," he said as we battled the crazed hordes in Foodway. He still hadn't lost that *Well. Here I am. Alone with Lucas. Now what?* look. We'd passed two Supercuts hair places on Broadway. I'd seen him eyeing them, but he hadn't stopped or said anything. "Frankly, Son, I was a little worried how you'd spend the week."

"It's been good," I said. I wished I'd brought a book with me. I could have read in the checkout lines. "I've been fine. It's been fun." Which was true. Till last night.

"I'm glad you've been getting out and about," he said. "I hope we can find a fresh turkey. Claire won't be pleased if we come home with a frozen one."

"Yeah, it's been good," I said again. "Book World's great."

"I'm glad," he said. "You always were a big reader. Which is good. Keeps you out of trouble."

It was like he was being Jolly Christmas Dad and I was Happy Christmas Son. He was doing better than I was, but neither of us was too great. It used to be like, *Wow, I can't wait to tell Dad that! I have to tell that to Dad!* I saved stuff up all week to tell him, back when he drove to Fairfield on Saturdays and took me out to lunch or to a game. Of course, I was nine then. Now all I saw was things I couldn't tell him. Like this grocery-cart road rage at Foodway, and how two ladies at the vegetable store almost got into a fistfight over chestnuts, and how even with four agents there was cash register gridlock at the Health Hut. Most of all, I couldn't tell him how bad I was feeling about Izzy.

"You can't go wrong with soap, Lucas," Dad said. We were in a bath store now. He'd finally caved and bought a frozen turkey. We'd picked the biggest one. It barely fit in our cart.

"What?" I said. "Excuse me?"

"For Claire and Phoebe," he said. "Lucas, are you with us? I thought you wanted to get gifts."

"Oh. Yeah. I do," I said. "That's a good idea, Dad. Thanks."

I got soap baskets for Claire and Phoebe both, and a soap-on-a-rope for Dad, too, when he wasn't looking. And I found a pail filled with bath toys for Calvin.

"So, you feeling a little cheerier now that the gift problem is solved?" he said as we lugged the stuff home.

"Yeah. Thanks, Dad."

The frozen turkey was less stiff than we were.

Claire pulled Dad aside when we got back. "So how'd your walk with Lucas go? You guys do okay together?" I heard her say.

"Fine, I guess," he said. "It went okay. You know . . ."

"Any calls for me?" I asked. I wasn't waiting just for Izzy. Mom had said she'd call today.

"Not yet," Claire said. She was upset about the turkey. "I knew we should have gotten it early. It's hard as a rock, Charles! What'd you do, buy the biggest one you could find? It's never going to thaw."

"It'll thaw," Dad said. "I promise. We'll put it in a bathtub full of water. It'll be fine."

"Yes, you do need to bake with Lucas," I heard her telling Phoebe as Dad and I filled the bathtub. "You can see he isn't having an easy time today. I'm sure he misses his mom. You know how it is when you're waiting for your dad to call." I didn't hear Phoebe's answer. All I heard was Claire saying, "I don't want to hear that, Phoebe. He always calls. And Lucas could use some cheering up and a little company."

"Lucas, you know every time you yawn, you get your germs in the cookie batter," Phoebe said almost as soon as we got started. I'd wanted to stay in my room and read, but Claire had coaxed me out. Calvin was in the kitchen with us. Calvin and Tinkerbell. Tinkerbell had been following me around all day, trying to get his nose in my fishy pocket.

I didn't have the energy to argue with Phoebe. "Sorry."

"Lucas, you're making all Santas. We have Santas, stars, trees, and bells. I have a system going here. We're supposed to have the same number of each kind." She had a system for stringing popcorn, too: three cranberries, three pieces of popcorn, three cranberries. And for poinsettias: one white, one pink, one red. And for wrapping presents. And tying bows.

What, you think someone's gonna say, "Sorry, I don't want this present! Forget it. It's got the same wrapping paper as my other one!" or, *"Take this back! It's got a messy bow!" Nobody cares, Phoebe! It doesn't matter how you tie the bow!*

I didn't say that. But Izzy would have.

Tink had finally figured out that there was no fish in my pocket, and moved on to untying Phoebe's ribbons the instant she got them tied.

"Tinkerbell, stop that!" She grabbed him and dumped him out the door. "I thought Tink hated you, Lucas! Mother!" she called. "Would you please get Calvin and Tinkerbell out of here? They're pestering us. Calvin, go away! Lucas, you gave him all that dough to play with. Of course he doesn't want to leave. Look at him. Ick! He's got dough blobs on his hat."

By dinnertime Izzy still hadn't called. Mom hadn't either. Claire was right. I missed Mom. Even if it was annoying that she still hadn't called. The only good thing was that no one had mentioned my hair.

"Would you mind a lot if I didn't go to church with you guys?" I asked Dad during dinner. "Would it be okay if I stayed here?"

I tried reading after they left for church, but I couldn't keep my mind on it, so I did some more work on my word list.

- bulbous
- blob
- dork
- vestibule
- sputum
- gizzard
- nozzle
- quality time

- chunky
- behave yourself
- hissy fit
- no way, José
- curdle
- vegan

I could have added a million Phoebe things to my "I Hate It When . . ." list, but I was depressed enough without seeing them in writing.

The phone rang. It was Mom.

"Merry Christmas, sweetheart! How is it there? How you doing? You surviving? Because this place is fabulous! You would love it. The water is so unbelievable. We have to come back here!" She sounded so excited.

"I'm surviving," I said.

"Did that tin of popcorn I ordered get there okay? The store promised it'd arrive in time for Christmas. They promised it would be really big."

"It's fine. We strung some and hung it on the tree."

"That's great!" she said.

"Yeah." I wished I could sound more excited. I wished I could tell her everything. "It was good here for a while," I said. "It's just . . ."

"Well, you won't be there much longer, Lucas. And then you'll be home. Try to keep your sense of humor. And have a good Christmas, okay, sweetheart? DTIP. Listen, these calls from the hotel phone cost an arm and a leg, so we'll keep this short."

I wished I were home now.

After I got off, I alphabetized the lists. I ate some of the popcorn. I'd just gotten the atlas down to look for Lapland when the intercom rang.

"There's a gentleman on his way up to see you," the door-man said.

"They're not here," I said.

"That's what I told him. I said the Grahams were out for the evening. He insisted he was here for you, so I sent him up."

My heart leaped.

"Is he old and short?" I said. "Was he wearing a toupee?"

"I try not to make judgments like that," he said, "but yeah, it looked like a toupee to me."

If it wasn't for the toupee, I wouldn't have recognized him. Izzy looked as if he'd shrunk overnight. His eyes were dull, with brown, wrinkly pouches under them. His shoulders sagged. Even his green jacket had lost its shine. "Izzy, are you okay?" I said. "What's going on?"

"It's over," he said. "I came to say good-bye." It sounded like it took all his energy to move his mouth.

"Good-bye?" My stomach dropped.

"I quit," he said. "I quit the bureau. I'm finished." He turned to go. "Leaving," he said. "Something had to give, and what gave was me."

"No!" I pushed him into the apartment. He looked around nervously. "It's okay," I said. "They're at church. I'm here alone." I walked him to the living room. He sank into Dad's chair. Tink hissed, jumped off, and ran away.

"So, what happened?" I said after I'd brought Izzy a glass of water.

He shrugged. "I told them the same things I told you. They didn't want to hear it. So I said, 'Good riddance to bad rubbish.' And they said, 'Who you calling rubbish, Rubbish?' and changed the locks on my room. They banned me from the passages, took my key to the Repository, took my user name, my password, my access code, my key card. They even cut up my fitness club membership. And you know what the Big Cheese said to me? He said, 'It's about time you're putting down your sword, Gribitz. This isn't a crusade. It's just a job.'" He laughed harshly. "Just a job! Like he could know. Like any of them have any idea."

I was scared he might cry. "You want a sugar cookie?" I said. "Or a pecan bar? We baked."

"I was never going for annoyance free," he said. "That's not possible. It's not even good. If nothing annoyed us, the world would never get better. If we weren't annoyed, how would we know we were alive? All I was ever trying for was livable, where everyone's not always grouchy and irritable and irked and frazzled and ready to explode. And I could have—"

"You're not in Lapland," I said. "That's something."

He didn't seem to hear me. "You never wondered why someone of my caliber had such a puny territory? One bookstore? Not even a whole chain? I covered all of Manhattan at one time. I thought I might get the state. Oh yes, Lucas, I had big dreams. Aaah"—he made a face—"what am I doing? You don't want to get me started."

"Yeah, I do." I sat down on the couch.

"You probably didn't even know I invented the earplug. Banished the poison ivy from Central Park. Signed the Raisin Removal Order—"

"I hate raisins!" I said.

"They overturned that one," he said. "But I did a lot in my day." He sighed. "Funny, isn't it? One minute you're in. The setup's not ideal. It's a pain in the patoot. You grouse and gripe and carry on. But you're used to it. You deal. Then, *boom*! Everything changes. You thought you knew what was what, and it turns out you know zip." He looked at me. "You're nodding like you know what I'm talking about."

"Yup." He'd just described what it had felt like when Mom and Dad split up. If I thought about that now, I'd feel even worse. "What are you going to do, Izzy?"

"I don't know. All I can tell you is this old horse has put his sword down. He's putting himself out to pasture." He got to his feet. "Have a nice life, kiddo. Merry Christmas."

"No!" I hated that old-man shrug of his. I couldn't stand this sighing. I jumped up. "You're talking like those rodential retreads fired you. They didn't fire you! You quit! And what's this crapulent good-bye?" I shouted. "I just met you!"

"I should never have made Hildegund hop," he said, moving toward the door. "It was beneath me. I was showing off for you, if the truth be known."

I followed him. "I loved it. It was great!" A horrible thought struck me. "They didn't take the irkostat?"

"No." He snorted. "At least I did one thing right. It was under the rug."

"And you were able to get it back?"

"It's still there."

He pulled off his toupee and turned it over. The irkostat was Velcroed to the inside.

"That's brilliant!" I couldn't help laughing. I'd always figured he was bald. He had grizzly white hair all over his head. "Izzy, you're a genius!"

"Some genius. I can't even get the stupid gizmo to work right."

"It's not a gizmo!" I said. "It's the irkostat. And it's not stupid. It's great. And we can work on it together."

"And where am I gonna use it?" He put the toupee back on. "Come on, Lucas. Get it through your head. It's over."

"You told me we were just getting started. You said we'd barely scratched—"

"Anything I try, they'll know. There are thousands of agents. They all know me."

"They don't know me." That wasn't true. But I couldn't stand that everything had come apart and there was nothing I could do to fix it.

"Hey," he said. "You had a three-day apprenticeship. So it goes. It was fun while it lasted. Merry Christmas, my friend. It's been nice knowing you." He opened the door.

"Wait!" I grabbed his arm. "Izzy, can't I be your apprentice anyway?"

His mouth twisted. "Apprentice what? Apprentice has-been? Apprentice nobody? You would have made a fine one, kiddo. But let's face it. A failure doesn't need an apprentice."

CHAPTER 13

"*This sucks!*" *I said.* "*This really sucks. I don't* know where you're going. What if I need you?"

"Why would you need me?" Izzy was still holding the doorknob.

"Because my life is insufferably pestiferous?"

"Pestiferous?" He looked at the paintings, the furniture, the giant Christmas tree with piles of presents under it. "You've got a pretty hotsy-totsy life going here—"

"No, I don't." I hated how my voice sounded. "You don't know Phoebe and her crapulent cat." Which gave me an idea. "Tinkerbell!" I called. "Here, Tink! Here, Kitty, Kitty!"

"What are you doing, Lucas?" Izzy couldn't wait to leave. I could tell.

"You'll see. Come on, Tink! Tink get in here!"

"It's late. I'm tired. It's gonna be murder getting a cab on Christmas Eve—"

"They won't be back from church for another hour. Please? You've got to see this. It'll just take a minute. Psss, psss, psss! Tink, come smell my pants!"

Tinkerbell stalked to the front hall, looking from me to Izzy like, *This better involve food.*

"Can I see the irkostat a minute?"

Izzy groaned but took off his toupee again and handed the irkostat to me. "Why? You think I need to see a cat chase its tail—"

"No, you'll like this. It's funny," I said. Tinkerbell was giving me that *And you called me for what exactly?* look. Which was good. It meant he didn't remember. "Tink, stay there! Izzy, you watching?" I turned the small knob. It fell off. "Huh?" I said. "What is this?" Last time it was the big knob that fell off. I stuck it back on and turned again.

Tinkerbell began to rise.

"Izzy, look! He's levitating!" I'd been worried the Bureau had canceled Izzy's powers, but the irkostat still worked. And Tinkerbell was definitely on the rise.

I turned the knob again. He was level with my pants pocket. His nose twitched. He started sniffing.

"What if I give it another turn? Maybe it can make him fly! Izzy, wouldn't it be cool if he, like, flew around the room? Cats land on their feet. It can't hurt him!" I was practically hopping up and down. I wished Izzy looked more excited. "Izzy, did you know it could do that?"

"What I don't know could fill volumes," he said. But he let the door close.

I gave the knob another turn.

Tinkerbell started swimming through the air.

"Look at him, Izzy! Look what the irkostat made him do! He's doing the doggy paddle!"

Tinkerbell, three feet off the ground, dog-paddled across the foyer to the living room. He swam over to the Christmas tree, swatted a few balls, gave the popcorn-and-cranberry string a sniff, then snagged a pinecone elf by its stocking cap and dropped it on the floor. He paddled to the dining room table and hooked a flower out of the vase. Then he swam on to the kitchen, hovered over his bowl like a helicopter, and meowed as if to say, *Uh, guys? I'm here.*

"A Cat Aerial Locomotion function." Izzy shook his head. "Who'd have guessed?"

I turned the knob the other way. Tink landed neatly and started eating.

Bzzzzzzt! The irkostat went off.

"What's it doing?" I said.

Izzy frowned. "Same thing it's always doing. I must have left it in Detect mode. I'll turn it off."

"Why? Don't you want to find out what got it buzzing?"

He shrugged.

"Come on," I said. "Izzy, let's go see."

"Pushy, pushy . . ." He was starting to get grouchy. Grouchy was better than depressed.

The buzzing got louder. *Beep-BEE-bee-dee-BEE-bee-dee-BEEEEE!*

"Izzy!" I grabbed his arm again. "Come on!"

He held the irkostat in front of him. I followed him down the hall to Dad's bathroom.

Beedle-beep-beep-BEEDLE-beedle-beedle-deedle-dee!

He was staring at the turkey in the bathtub. "Lucas, may I ask you a question? Was that 'Turkey in the Straw'?"

I nodded.

"And before that? 'Be Kind to Your Web-Footed Friends'?"

I nodded again.

"We may have to add "fowl detector" to the irkostat's capabilities!"

I was so glad to hear him laugh, I didn't tell him turkeys didn't have webbed feet.

"Lucas," he said, "it would appear we haven't begun to

plumb the depths of this device, which gives new meaning to the words 'artificial intelligence.' The mind boggles. Or should I say gobbles?"

He was starting to sound like the old Izzy.

"Let's check the annoyance level in here," I said.

"You got it." He pressed some buttons and looked at it. "Not too bad. Four. Moderately exasperating. Strictly within normal range. As I said, your house is not exactly a hotbed of annoyance."

"Maybe not this room. Try in there!" I pointed toward Phoebe's bathroom.

We went in. There were retainer rubber bands on the sink, hairs in the sink, specks of glitter everywhere, and about a hundred bottles with their covers off, lined up like little Lucas booby traps.

He studied the irkostat and frowned. "You're right. This is bad," he said. "You are sharing a bathroom with someone profoundly annoying. Would you believe eight-point-three on the Gribitz scale?"

I looked at the irkostat. I couldn't see anything. "Where do you see that? Izzy, you never told me about the Gribitz scale."

"I just created it. What, you thought all this was etched in stone? This is a work in progress here. You're witnessing history in the making—"

Oh, yes. The old Izzy was definitely back!

Bee-bee-bee-BEEEE-BZZZZZZZZZZZZZZZZZZZZZZT!

"And now it's multitasking! Blinking and beeping at the same time! Lord love a duck, Lucas!" He pointed toward Phoebe's room. "We've found the annoyance epicenter—"

"Of the world?"

"Let's not get carried away. Of the apartment. I hesitate to set foot in there. It's a whopping nine-point-four!"

"It'd be ten if she were home!" I said.

"Your room, by contrast"—he was pointing the irkostat at my door—"is a veritable oasis. May I?"

"Sure," I said. "Go in."

We did. "I'm getting a four plus on your backpack, but that's natural. This item, however"—he aimed the irkostat at my hat, lying on the chair—"we're talking five-point-two to five-point-seven range: ridiculously irritating."

"I got it from the passages," I said.

"Why am I not surprised?" He picked it up and put it on, tied the earflaps under his chin, then looked at himself in the mirror. The orange, red, and yellow tassel was hanging in his eye. "I might have to up that to preposterously annoying." He made a face.

I didn't know if I was allowed to laugh.

"Then again"—he flipped the tassel back—"this annoyance business is a subtle one. There are two sides to every coin. The merest flip-flop changes preposterously annoying to annoyingly preposterous, and—oh, my goodness! Lucas!" An impish gleam came into his eye. "What do you think? You think the bureau pissants would recognize me with this bad boy on my head?" He waggled his eyebrows. "Think maybe I could slip into the passages with it?"

"Izzy!" I'd just had another idea. A scary idea. I said it anyway. "If I cut my hair, the pissants wouldn't recognize me, either. I could come with you." I checked my watch. I still had half an hour. He could help me. We could do it now. "Izzy, d'you know anything about cutting hair?"

"What's to know? It's long, you cut it off, it's short. You're not cutting your hair. We discussed it. You decided your hair was staying on your head."

"Yes, I know, but if it meant you could do your work again—"

"Hold on there, Lucas." He stopped smiling. "We've gotta get a grip here, you and me. I was joking."

"No, you weren't!" I said.

"Well, then, I should have been. I'm retired. Out of business. Remember? I threw in the towel. Kaput. *Finito.*" He ran a finger across his throat. "R.I.P."

"What?"

He took off my hat and dropped it on the chair.

"So, then . . . what?" I said. "The irkostat goes back under the rug?" My voice cracked. "Izzy, you just made a cat fly—"

"Not fly, Lucas. Swim."

"Whatever. You just invented the Gribitz scale."

"I've invented all sorts of things."

"Exactly! The earplug. The irkostat . . . I mean, unless we don't need it anymore. Unless the world's stopped being annoying, unless—"

He glared at me. "You know, you're starting to get on my nerves."

"You told me I was your apprentice," I said. "You said I could have made a fine one." I had to swallow. "I am a fine one!"

He didn't answer.

"So, then . . . what?" I said. "You're gonna leave?"

This lump in my throat was making me mad.

We stood there glaring at each other. Then he sat down on my bed.

"It's possible there's a scissors attachment on the irkostat," he said. "I could try to give it a mental message and find out." He pressed a bunch of buttons, then more buttons. A hatch I'd never seen opened. A nail clipper popped out. He groaned, put it in his pocket, and pressed more buttons. A tiny toothpick appeared. He snorted and kept pressing. Out came a folded-up pair of scissors.

"You're sure you're ready for this?" he said.

I definitely wasn't, but I nodded.

We went back to the bathroom. I sat down on the toilet. He draped a towel over me—Phoebe's towel, but I'd worry about that later—unfolded the scissors, and began to snip. Within minutes the floor was covered with hair.

"Oho! Look at this," he said. "The boy has eyebrows. And ears. Who knew?"

"Let me see!" I started to get up.

He pushed me back down. "Cool your jets." He kept snipping. The pile on the floor was getting deep. "Hmmm. Not bad. Not bad at all. I may have missed my calling here, Lucas. Take a look."

I hopped up and peered in the mirror. My hair had its same tufts and sprigs, but they were an inch long. Some maybe half an inch. "I look naked," I said. "I look six. I never knew I had such a tiny head."

"Turn around." He stepped back and looked me over. "It is a bit on the petite side," he said. "No visible lumps or bumps, though. And as for looking six"—he ripped his mustache off his face and held it under my nose—"a little facial hair could solve that. But that's a matter for another time. Speaking of which, how we doing?"

I checked my watch. "Oh, no!" They were due back in two minutes. "You'd better go!"

"You're right." He stuck the scissors in his pocket, grabbed the irkostat, and followed me to the kitchen.

"This way!" I said, opening the door to the service hall and showing him the back stairs. "You want to take the hat? You gonna be okay getting home?"

"Is Izzy Gribitz gonna be okay?" he called as he started down. "Is the sky blue? Is the ocean deep? Are annoyances rampant and getting more so by the minute?" He stopped, turned around, and saluted. "You're a most annoyingly persistent apprentice, Lucas. Keep the hat. I'll be in touch."

I'd barely swept the bathroom floor by the time they got home.

Phoebe started screaming when she saw me. "What happened to your *hair?*"

"I cut it," I told her.

"You certainly did," Dad said.

Claire was looking at me like, *I should say something nice. What would that be?*

Dad reached down and petted Tinkerbell, who was conked out on the couch, his head dangling over the side, snoring. "What made you decide to take matters into your own hands, so to speak? How'd you do it? How on earth did you do the back?"

"Uh. I don't know," I said. "I just did. It wasn't that hard, really."

I should have asked Izzy where he was going. He'd said he'd be in touch, but he hadn't said when or how soon. I wished I'd given him my lists.

"Be gentle, Calvin. Let Tinkerbell sleep. He's tired." Claire lifted Calvin away from Tinkerbell, then came over and patted at my hair. "You really didn't have to do that, Lucas. If you want, after we hang the Christmas stockings and get Calvin down, I can try to neaten—"

"I don't know," Dad said. "It gives him kind of a downtown look . . . like, what . . . I don't know . . . MTV or something."

"MTV? Dad!" Phoebe did her slump-sigh. "You've never even seen MTV. Nobody on MTV—"

"I knew you really wanted it cut for Christmas," I told Claire. "And since tomorrow's Christmas . . ."

Where did that come from? Lies never used to come so easily.

Claire looked at Dad and then kissed my ear. "It was a very sweet thing to do, Lucas. Maybe you'd like to give us a hand later filling Calvin's stocking."

So then, it wasn't a bad lie.

"Suck-up," Phoebe whispered as soon as they left. "And did anyone ever tell you you've got a teensy head?"

But not even Phoebe could ruin my mood tonight. Izzy wasn't in Lapland. Izzy had come to me for help. I'd helped him.

CHAPTER 14

Calvin woke me at six thirty the next morning.

"Woof? Woof, woof?" There was chocolate on his face, he had on the hat and his pajamas, and he was dancing up and down, carrying his Christmas stocking in one hand, and in the other . . . was that strange-looking rusty brownish black thing Izzy's mustache?

I sat up. "Calvin! Where'd you find that?"

"Woof?" His eyebrows rose. He smiled. "Iz?"

"*What?*" I took the mustache from him. "Calvin, what'd you say?"

His smile got even bigger. "Irk?"

And I'd wondered about Izzy's powers?

"Okay. We go around. Each person opens one thing at a time," Phoebe said. "Who goes first?" We were all in the living room with blueberry muffins Claire had baked, and our hot chocolate and coffee. "Lucas, you just dropped a blueberry on our white rug."

"Lucas goes first," Dad said. "Lucas"—he pulled a big red-wrapped package from under the tree—"open this one."

It was the big box from Mom. Calvin clapped, danced around, and barked as I ripped the paper. Books. Sci fi, a major stack. Excellent. Dad and Claire said things like, "Oh, that looks great. Good choice!" as I passed them around. Phoebe said, "Oh, boring! Books," as usual only loud enough for me to hear. As if her gifts weren't snores: Clothes. More clothes. Fluffy slippers. The soap from me.

I got slippers too. Also pajamas. I had to remember to put *people who make you model the gifts they bought you* on my list.

Calvin thought opening presents was the greatest thing ever. He cheered and clapped for our gifts as much as for his own.

Claire gave him a stuffed squirrel. "What do squirrels say?" she asked him.

Calvin gave me the exact same look as when he'd said "Iz," turned to Claire, and said, "Woof!"

"No! Only dogs go 'Woof,' honey," Claire said. "Squirrels say . . ."

"Lucas, *you're* from the, quote, country," Phoebe said. "What *do* squirrels say?"

Air quotes had to go on the list, too.

Dad got me a Frisbee for Aslan and a very cool computer role-playing game.

"We can install it on my machine if you want," he said.

"You never let *me* put anything on your computer," Phoebe said.

"I'm saying that so we can all try it later, if we feel like it," Dad said. "And your mother and I have to work tomorrow and Friday. I don't want Lucas to be bored."

I was hoping we could try it. But Dad and Claire got into a whole dinner argument.

"You were supposed to keep adding water to the bathtub," Dad said as he dug around in the turkey's insides, first with a long fork and then with a knife.

"I thought you *did,*" Claire said.

"I thought *you* were doing that," he said.

"Well, you didn't make that clear. And now the giblets are still frozen inside. It's totally full of ice."

"I'm aware of that," Dad said. "And do we have to go through this every time your family comes?"

"We don't go through this," Claire said. "I always get a fresh turkey."

"They didn't have a fresh turkey. Honey, it's not as if the president and the first lady are coming for dinner. It's just your family."

"Just?" Claire said. "What is that supposed to mean?"

Giblets was going on my annoying-word list. Along with *family.*

The first ones to arrive were Uncle Jerry and Aunt Laura and their daughter. Aunt Laura was Claire's twin. Cousin Alexandra was Phoebe Junior. Except that unlike Phoebe, she liked me. I couldn't decide if that was good in an annoying way or annoying in a good way or just annoying.

"How old are you?" Alexandra was eleven. "Where do you live?" Alexandra lived in New Jersey. "Do you like Connecticut?" She hated New Jersey. "What's your favorite group?" Hers was the Beat Street Boys.

Her questions didn't stop till Claire's mom and dad arrived.

"And you must be the famous Lucas," Grandpa George said, shaking my hand. "The doorman asked me to give this to you." He handed me a shopping bag.

"Ooh, what's in it?" Alexandra peered in the bag. "Let me see."

It was a box wrapped in silver paper.

"Open it!" Alexandra said.

It was a shoe box.

"Shoes?" Alexandra said. "Who sent you shoes?"

It wasn't shoes. It was a shrink-wrapped fruitcake.

My heart started pounding.

"That must be from your mom," Grandma Jean said. "We heard she was in the Caribbean. These days you can order anything from anywhere. It's remarkable. Do you think she ordered it on the Internet?"

"I hate fruitcake!" Phoebe said.

"Ha! Ha! Who doesn't?" Uncle Jerry had one of those booming laughs. "Everyone hates fruitcake. But you know what they say. It's not Christmas without fruitcake."

I tore the envelope open and, turning away so Alexandra couldn't see, read the note:

> *Surely you have laundry to do.*
> *I'd rather be annoyance sweeping, but I'll be doing wash all afternoon, if you get my drift.*
>
> *P.S. Any idea how hard it was to find one of these with no raisins????*

No signature. It didn't need one.

Sitting through present opening was torture. Dinner was worse. Alexandra sat next to me. "Do you like the city?" she asked. "Do you play an instrument? What's your favorite TV show? Who's your favorite Beat Street Boy?"

"No offense, Mother," Phoebe was saying. "This turkey is slimy."

"It's not slimy." Claire gave her a dirty look. "It's fine. It's not dried out, is all."

"Ha! Ha! Just put more gravy on it, Phoebe," Uncle Jerry said.

"The gravy is delicious, Claire," Grandma Jean said.

"It is the tiniest bit pink, Claire," Aunt Laura said.

"Pink? It's bright red." Phoebe held up a slice. "Red. See?"

"Ha, ha! It's al dente, is all," said Uncle Jerry.

"My slice is fine," Grandpa George said. "Try a different one, Phoebe."

"I think it's delicious," Grandma Jean said.

"Everything's delicious, Claire," Aunt Laura said.

"Absolutely delicious," Grandma Jean said.

I didn't know if it was delicious or not delicious. I didn't know if these people were truly annoying, or if I was annoyed because I needed to find Izzy, and I didn't know if he meant the laundry room here in the basement, and if he was already down there waiting for me, and how I could get down there with everyone here, and how I was going to survive dinner.

I survived dinner. I helped clear the table. But I turned down Dad's offer to watch the game, and as soon as Claire and her mom and Aunt Laura took Calvin for a walk, and Phoebe and Alexandra went to her room, I stuck my lists in my pocket and slipped out the back door.

CHAPTER 15

"I told you I'd be in touch." Izzy was pushing a large janitor broom around the laundry room. "The night went perfectly. I set the irkostat to detect everything that came through the door—"

"You spent the night here?" I looked at the big, windowless room with its cement floor, cinder block walls, row of hard blue plastic chairs, folding tables, and clanking dryers.

"It was fine," he said. "I fixed the pay phone. A washing machine overflowed and I mopped it up. I swept the entire basement. Not exactly the annoyance sweep I had in mind, but as I've said, you're either part of the solution or part of the problem. We correct what we can, and we use the means at our disposal." He leaned his broom against the wall. "How's the level up where you are?"

"Ridiculously irritating." I couldn't stop smiling. "Oh, by the way . . ." I handed him his mustache.

"Ah, yes." He stuck it on.

I had to find out how he did that. When I tried it on myself, it fell off on the floor.

I pulled the pad from my pocket. "I brought my annoyance lists," I said. "If you want to see."

"If I want to see?" he said. "Of course I want to see." I handed him the pad. He turned pages. "What'd you do, alphabetize them?"

"Why?" I said. "Is that annoying?"

"Not to me. This is excellent! So you don't care for air quotes, alarm clocks, beepers, birdcall clocks, candied yams, computer crashes, garbage bags that break, glitter, gum, hamster wheels, hat head, hiccups, hives, honking horns, or knock-knock jokes? Neither do I!" He beamed and kept reading: "'I hate it when people

"act sarcastic, as in 'And . . . ?' or 'Is that your final answer?';
bite the bottom off your ice cream cone;
bite their nails;
count their Christmas presents;
count everyone else's Christmas presents;
dot their *i*'s with little hearts (guess who????)."

"I agree! Those little hearts drive me bonkers!" He went on reading to himself, nodding and laughing. "This is great stuff you got here, Lucas. Right on the money! How'd you come up with all these?" He read aloud again, still chuckling:

"Say 'Is that what you're wearing?' or 'What were you thinking?' or 'You can't think that looks good?';
say 'Have a good one!';
say 'Uh-huh, uh-huh' when they're not listening;
say 'We'll see';
say 'No offense' and then say something offensive;
say 'What's going on? Did you see that? Huh? What happened?' during movies;

spit;

shake soda bottles;

spell their names in cutesy ways (Fibi!!!!!!);

think they're always right;

watch you eat."

"It was easy!" I said. "I can do more, too. I can keep adding—"

"Indubitably!" He looked up. One of the washing machines had started to make glubbing noises, like Tinkerbell getting ready to vomit. He pointed the irkostat at it and pressed buttons. It glubbed louder. "Why isn't this working, Lucas? I've set it to Correct. It's supposed to be correcting. Why isn't it correcting—"

Bzzzzzt! Bzzzzt!

"Now what?" He scurried to the door and peeked out, then ran back. "Oh, no. It's *her*! She just got off the elevator."

"Hildegund? She tracked you here?"

"No"—he raised his eyebrow—"Madam Kidney."

I giggled. "Gladys?"

"The one and only. And she's singing." He cupped his hand to his ear. "Hear that?"

I did now: "I'm a little teapot, short and stout. Here is my . . ."

"Time to hop." He pushed more buttons on the irkostat, and we ran toward a door at the end of the laundry room.

"Where are we going?" The singing was getting louder. "I only have a few minutes," I said. "I had to sneak away."

"Don't worry," he said. "I've set Detect to give us the all clear once she's gone."

He opened the door. The smell of onion rings hit me.

"The passages? I thought you couldn't be down there

anymore," I said as we stepped onto the landing. "Isn't it too dangerous?"

"Nah. The bureau's off today, which of course is colossally misguided. Anyone with the brains of a flea beetle knows the annoyance factor spikes on Christmas. But that's not my problem anymore, is it, Lucas? I've jumped clear. I'm on my own. What am I talking about?" He patted me. "I'm not on my own at all." He pulled a mutilated-looking hot dog from his pocket, squatted, and wedged it in the door. "I knew this Tofu Pup would come in handy someday."

We started down the stairs. "So Gladys is an agent?" I asked. That explained a lot.

"Lord, no." He rolled his eyes. "Unless they've started a Baby-sitting Division."

"It's kind of sad she's doing her laundry on Christmas," I said.

"Sad?" he said. "I find her unspeakably irritating. Which is what I told her this morning as she came in with her laundry bag of fluffy pink unmentionables and her absurd nursery rhymes. I said, 'Well, well, our paths cross once again. Madam Kidney, as I live and breathe.'"

I laughed. "Uh-oh! Did she hear you?"

"No, fortunately for me, my irkostatic friend here seemed to be stuck in Mute mode. Otherwise I might have gotten a rap on the knuckles, or possibly a time-out. She did, however, hand me a tissue and suggest I blow my nose. What?" He glared at me. "You find that funny? Do I look three to you? This is Izzy Gribitz, former Higher-up of the Annoyance Bureau of Greater New York. Annoyance eradicator *extraordinaire*. And no, Lucas, for your information, I am not afraid of her!"

"Yeah, well, if you think *she's* bad," I said, "you should meet Phoebe."

"Phagh! Compared with Madam Kidney, Phoebe is small potatoes."

"To you, maybe." Though down here, with him, Phoebe *was* seeming like a smaller potato than she had a while ago.

"Well—" he stopped walking—"I'm lucky she didn't hear me, but I had fun saying it irregardless. That's not a word, by the way, Lucas. Don't use it. I only use it to annoy myself when I fear I'm having too good a time, if you get my drift. I wouldn't want to lose my edge."

I nodded. "I loved your fruitcake. I don't mean eating it—"

"You didn't happen to bring a hunk? I'm feeling a mite peckish." I shook my head. We were at the bottom of the stairs now. He opened the door, and we stepped out into the passage. He sniffed the air. "Delightful down here, isn't it?"

It was nice. I liked onion rings. This section had tiny ferns poking up between the paving stones, and mushrooms sprouting from cracks in the walls.

"How long has this been here?" I said as we started walking. The passage was deserted. "How long has the Annoyance Bureau been around, anyway?" The paving stones looked ancient. There were a lot of doors. "Do regular people know about the passages? If there are doors everywhere, can anyone just open one and walk in?" I glanced behind us. "Like Madam Kidney?"

"There's always been an Annoyance Bureau in one form or another," he said. "This is merely its most recent incarnation. And the doors are always there. It's just that most people are too busy doing what they're doing to see them."

"So why do I see them?"

"What can I tell you?" he said. "It's a gift. In every sense of the word." He stopped walking and looked at me. "You said a mouthful last night. Per usual. You got me to see that life goes on, that there is life after the Annoyance Bureau. I'm going independent, Lucas. And I can use a hand, if you're still interested."

"I'm interested!" I said.

"*Wunderbar!*" His eyes were shining. "The possibilities are endless. All it takes is vision and imagination. We've got the will. We've got the way. The way being the irkostat. We just need to find our niche. We could be gazillionaires. Not that we give two hoots for the money . . . we're walking east, by the way. If we went west, we'd be headed under the Hudson River. Can't say I've done that. I like New Jersey as well as the next guy, but . . ."

"My stepcousin's from New Jersey," I said. "Alexandra." I wrinkled my nose. "She's up there now."

"You don't like her?"

I thought about it. "I don't *dis*like her." She was actually a little nice. "But she's pretty annoying."

"Most people are pretty annoying. Some are extremely annoying. Some are off the map. Me, for example."

I laughed. He had to be a ten on the Gribitz scale. Ten plus-plus. "It doesn't bother me!" I said.

"My point exactly. It's all in whether they push your buttons. I recognize that there are certain aspects of Lucas J. Graham, just to pick someone else at random, that could get under certain people's skin. A certain noodgy persistence and persistent pleasantness. Of course, we don't like those people—"

Beep-bee-beep-bee-beeee-BEEEEEEEE!

"There's our all clear," he said, pushing a button to stop the irkostat. "It's safe to return. Madam Kidney hath departed."

I hated to turn back.

As we reached the door to my building I saw a mischievous gleam in his eye. "Oho! How's this for an idea, Lucas?" he said as we started up the stairs. "And don't ask me how we do it. I haven't gotten that far. We take the annoyances we've eradicated, we distill them to their pure, unadulterated essence, and we bottle it. We'll call it '*Eau de* Annoyance.'" I laughed. "But would that be an attractant or a repellent? Stop laughing, Lucas. I've got more ideas than you can shake a finger at. Here's another one. We program the irkostat to play 'I'm a Little Teapot,' and then tip the offending party over . . . see that? Unspeakable or no, Madam Kidney is inspiring me. Wait a minute." We were at the door to the basement now. "What is this?" He suddenly sounded upset. "What's going on here?"

I ran up beside him. He was pointing to the door. It was closed tight. The Tofu Pup was squashed flat. There was no knob. No handle. We were locked in.

CHAPTER
16

"What are you going to do?" I said as Izzy pointed the irkostat and pressed a bunch of buttons. Nothing happened. He pressed more buttons. Still nothing. "Come on, baby!" he said. "Correct for me now. You fixed the pay phone for me. If you did it once, you can do it again."

"Once? It's corrected only once?" I checked my watch. I'd been gone half an hour. They had to have noticed. He was still pushing buttons. I should have left a note. "If Correct doesn't work, how will we get out? Should we go down and look for another exit? Can we call for help?"

"Quiet, Lucas. You're messing up my mental messages." He closed his eyes and pressed more buttons.

The door popped open.

"Lord love a duck! Hallelujah!" He kissed the irkostat. "See, Lucas!" he cried as we walked through into the basement. "It corrected. It came through for me!" He checked to make sure no one was coming. Then we started for the laundry room. "See that? Except when it doesn't, it works perfectly."

"Good thing!" I said. The laundry room was empty. We

went in. I checked my watch again. "I should get going."

"This is so puzzling." He sat down and looked the irkostat over. "Detect works fine; Inspect works brilliantly; the range of tunes continues to surprise me. If only this confounded Correct function weren't so flaky. And this is not a case of 'Garbage in, garbage out.' My mental messages are crystal clear—"

"You keep bringing up these mental messages," I said.

"That's how it knows what to correct," he said. "And this is what's so maddening. We can't correct without the Correct function. Let me see that list of yours again."

I handed it to him.

"'People who talk about you behind your back,'" he read. "'Not-too-bright, sneaky bullies; smirking; sneering; snort-laughing.' Think about it, Lucas! Think how you'll feel if we can correct even one of these. . . ."

"The irkostat could change how people act?" I stopped thinking about Dad and Claire wondering where I'd disappeared to, Phoebe hoping I'd fallen out the window. I sat down next to him. "How is that possible?"

"The mind boggles, doesn't it?"

"Let me take another look at it."

He put the irkostat in my hand. It still looked like an oversize remote with forty-eight blank buttons, bizarre knobs, and a blank screen.

"Okay," I said. "Show me how it's supposed to work."

"Simple. There are function buttons and number buttons. To set the functions, which is to say INSPECT, DETECT, PROTECT, CORRECT—"

"Why aren't the buttons labeled?" I said. "Why isn't there a display? How do you see the menu?"

"That I can't tell you," he said. "But if you know what you're doing . . ." He pointed to a button. "This is CORRECT right here. I press it, and then I transmit the mental message. Then"—he turned the irkostat over—"I press POUND. Then I hit STAR, five, nine, then ENTER—"

"Wait. Slow down! I don't see a star button. Or a pound button." Maybe you needed powers to find any of them. "Izzy, do you see a star, or ENTER, or a five or a nine?"

"No," he said.

"What? So then how do you know what you're doing? How does it work? This makes no sense."

"I've thought that many times," he said. "I also never grasped why it had to be this complicated. I mean, forty-eight buttons? Come on. Unless it was that—"

"What? Izzy! You don't know how it works either? You have to know. You invented it. You made it."

It took too long for him to answer. "Actually, I didn't. The concept was mine, but I'm unfortunately not engineerically inclined, so I contracted it out. To a retired engineer."

"What?"

"I wish you'd stop saying 'what,' Lucas! And don't look at me like that. It was a bad move. I see it now. But he sounded as if he knew what he was doing."

I checked my watch again, put the irkostat in his hand, and stood up. "Izzy, where can I find you tomorrow?"

"Right here," he said. "I was thinking I'd stay—"

"In the laundry room?"

"Yeah. If that's all right with you. I'll take my chances with Madam K."

"Okay," I said. "Tomorrow we'll go find this guy. Not to hurt your feelings, but you could be doing something wrong, something simple even, and this engineer can explain it to us. Or explain how it's put together. Maybe if we know how it's put together . . ."

I turned to leave.

He grabbed my arm. "Lucas, do you want the bad news or the bad news? This retired engineer, I'm embarrassed to report, worked for the Annoyance Bureau. He is also the late, lamented engineer. Our engineer is, regrettably, defunct."

So much for changing how people acted. So much for my lists.

His grip tightened. "I'd be more depressed about it, Lucas, if I didn't have you."

"Me?" What was he talking about? I was a kid. I had no powers.

"Take it with you tonight," he said. "Study it. Apply that noodgy persistence, which I recognize as brilliance. Lucas." He looked right in my eyes. "Please."

He'd asked for my help before. But he'd never looked at me like this.

"I can't get back until tomorrow," I said.

"I'll be waiting," he said.

The dishwasher was still going when I opened the kitchen door and stepped back into the apartment. Calvin, Claire, and the others were still out; Dad and Grandpa George were still watching the game; Uncle Jerry had corked off in the chair; behind Phoebe's door the same CD was playing. The irkostat was in my pocket. Izzy'd turned off the beep and tested it before giving it to me. "I've been in your apartment," he'd said. "The annoyances we logged up there, the beeping would keep you up all night."

Inspect, detect, protect, correct.

What made him think I could fix it? What made him think I was brilliant?

I loved that he thought I was brilliant.

Inspect: It found annoyances. It beeped when it heard

them. It played songs—sometimes that fit the annoyance, sometimes not. Or was that Detect? It had definitely
detected me at Trims for Tykes. It had absolutely detected
me the time Dad called the help line. It had led Izzy to the
apartment.

Or had Izzy done those things himself? Without the irkostat?

I couldn't remember ever seeing it protect. And where
did measuring annoyance levels fit in? Was that another -ect,
or was it something else? The irkostat had given us all those
readings, but I'd never seen the readout.

I lay on my bed examining it, staring at it, turning it over
and over, looking for a clue. There was none.

Correct made no sense either. Izzy'd said this was only
the second time Correct had worked, but I'd seen the irkostat unstick that kid's jacket from his braces. I'd seen it make
the pile of books disappear. Except that hadn't been the
irkostat. Izzy had snapped his fingers. So then maybe this
was all Izzy's mental messages—Izzy's powers. Maybe the
irkostat wasn't flaky. Maybe Izzy only thought it worked.
Maybe the irkostat was a hunk of plastic.

No. I'd seen the Mute button work. Izzy had been
nowhere around when I'd turned the knob and Tinkerbell
had whirled. I'd seen Tinkerbell swim. I'd seen Gladys
squeal. I'd seen Hildegund hop.

I couldn't believe he thought I'd solve this. There was no
solving this. I didn't know why I kept staring at it.

I was still staring at it when Alexandra stuck her head in.
"What's up?" she said.

I shoved it under the pillow. "Nothing much."

"You look busy," she said.

"I am." Maybe the -ects belonged to the bureau, not the
irkostat. No. Wrong. Izzy had left the bureau, and he still

had his powers. But maybe he'd lost some of them—
Correct, for example. Maybe that was the problem.

"What are you doing?" She came in but stayed over by
the door.

"Nothing." There could be more than four *-ects*. Select?
Direct? Perfect? Maybe each button was a different *-ect*
function.

Alexandra was staring at me. She really did look amaz-
ingly like Phoebe. "You look so serious," she said. "You look
like your head's gonna explode."

"No, I'm just thinking," I said. "I have something I need
to figure out."

"Oh. Yeah. Thinking." She didn't sound like she was
mocking me. "I do that too." She looked at the new books
piled up on the desk. "You got these for Christmas? Can I
see?"

"Sure. Why not?" Reject? Collect? Disinfect? Would
more *-ects* explain anything?

"Oh, cool." She was already looking through the books.
"Are you just into sci fi, or do you read fantasy? I read a lot
of fantasy."

"Like what?" I was getting nowhere with the *-ects* anyway.

"Alex!" The bathroom door opened. Phoebe had her
arms crossed and her head tipped to one side. She and Alex
didn't look nearly as alike as I'd thought. The shape of their
faces, and their hair and eyes might be the same, but
Phoebe had a sneery mouth and sarcastic eyebrows. Even
her chin was mean.

Bzzzzzzzt!

The irkostat wasn't supposed to be beeping. I'd seen Izzy
turn it off. He'd tested it on Gladys's underwear before he
let me have it.

"Alex," Phoebe said again.

Bzzzzzzzt! I was pretty sure I knew where the Beep button was. I pressed it.

"Hello, Dolly, Well, hello, Dolly . . ."

Uh-oh. The irkostat either had a radio in it, or it was singing. No. It was talking:

"If you wish to speak to a relationship specialist, please press or say 'one'. . ."

Alexandra and Phoebe didn't seem to hear it.

"Alex. I thought we were going to do our nails," Phoebe was saying.

"We are," Alexandra said. "I'm just saying hi to Lucas. Lucas, did you read *The Dark Is Rising*?"

A "Good-bye" came from under the pillow, and then the sound of the AOL slamming door.

Alex and Phoebe might not hear it yet, but I couldn't take any chances. I lay down so as much of me as possible covered the pillow. I could still feel the irkostat vibrating.

"Yeah, I read that. It was really good," I said. "I've read all of hers."

"Yes, Lucas is a very big reader," Phoebe said. "That's what he does. He reads."

The AOL door slammed again. The irkostat vibrated harder.

Phoebe came into my room and took Alexandra's arm. "Come on. We don't have that much time—"

"*Bweeet!* This is a test of the emergency broadcasting system. In the event of a real emergency . . ."

They had to have heard that.

"Eeooh." Phoebe's nose wrinkled. "What's that smell? It smells like rotten eggs." She fanned the air. It did stink in here suddenly. "Lucas, is that you?"

No. It's you. I wished I had the nerve to say that.

The irkostat was trying to vibrate itself to smithereens. Either that or it was trying to get out from under me.

"I don't smell anything," Alexandra said. "Lucas, did you read—"

"Come on, Alex"—Phoebe took Alexandra's arm—"it reeks in here. You don't actually *like* him?" she said loudly enough so I could hear as they went out through the bathroom.

"Yeah. Why not? He's cool," Alexandra said.

I sat up.

"Cool? Lucas? You can't be serious."

I was sure Phoebe was staying in the bathroom on purpose so I could hear.

"I like him," I heard Alexandra say. "He's interesting."

I waited to hear if she'd add anything. Phoebe didn't give her a chance. "Well, yeah, if you mean like a specimen—"

I didn't need the irkostat to sing or talk or vibrate. I needed to find the Mute button that would mute Phoebe.

"Shut up, Phoebe!" I yelled.

Whoa. Maybe I'd found a Lucas activator button. But the Lucas activator button, if there was one, only worked once, because when she called back, "Uh, Lucas? Do you always spy on girls when they're in the bathroom?" I couldn't think of anything to say.

No. I could think of lots of things. I just couldn't say them.

Izzy was wrong. Phoebe was not small potatoes. Phoebe was a big, fat pile of pestilentially putrid potatoes. We needed to get this thing fixed. Urgently.

The irkostat had settled down, even if I hadn't, when there was another knock, this time on the hall door.

The door opened. "How's it going?" Dad said.

"Okay." I shoved the irkostat in the drawer.

"Am I disturbing you?" Dad had that stiff, fidgety look.

"No." I tried to look normal. Which would have been hard even if Phoebe hadn't come in and the irkostat hadn't run amok. I could feel myself stiffening up too. "It's fine."

"So, how's your Christmas going?" He stepped into the room. He didn't seem to smell anything. "You having a good time? I notice you're in here by yourself. You getting along with everyone okay? They're saying nice things about you."

"They are?"

"They absolutely are. They're so happy to have finally met you."

What about Phoebe? I felt like asking him. While I was at it, I should ask how he could stand living in the same house with her, how someone like that was allowed to live.

"I was just telling George how I've been working so much that you and I have hardly gotten any time together. And I started thinking"—he stepped closer—"what do you say we have lunch tomorrow?"

"Really? Just you and me?" Could that be fun, I wondered, or would it be Turkey Walk II?

"Yeah." He nodded. "I was thinking you'd come down to my office and we'd grab a bite. You feel up to taking the subway? Because I can give you directions." He was looking like he really wanted me to say yes.

I'd never been on the subway by myself. On the other hand, I'd found my way from the bureau coffee shop to Calvin's doctor's office through the passages. "Yeah. Okay," I said. It wasn't as if I was having any irkostat breakthroughs. "Yeah. Sure." I'd tell Izzy tomorrow morning when I went down. "Okay. That sounds good!"

"Good." He patted my shoulder. "Very good." Then he hugged me.

It was good.

Later, when everyone was leaving, Alexandra handed me a piece of paper with her e-mail address. "You can let me know if you've read anything cool, and I'll tell you what I'm reading," she said.

"Cool," I said. I wrote down my e-mail address. Phoebe was giving me snide looks, but I ignored them because Alexandra was giving me friendly looks. Alexandra was nice. I might be nowhere with the irkostat, but an e-mail from Alexandra seemed somewhat good to me.

CHAPTER 17

"*You're not nervous about going downtown by* yourself, are you?" Dad asked the next morning when I came into the dining room.

"No, I'm okay with it."

"Excellent." Dad poured me some juice and showed me the instructions he'd written out for getting to his office. He'd even drawn a map.

"Calvin and I would be happy to take Lukey down," Gladys called from the kitchen.

Uh, no thank you, Madam Kidney. I hoped Izzy'd been okay without the irkostat. Taking the subway felt a lot easier than telling him we were nowhere. I'd stayed up really late last night hoping for something brilliant. Anything.

"I'll be fine, Gladys," I called back to her.

"Okeydokey, Lukey Dukey!"

You'd think that would set off the irkostat. But after its singing episode last night it hadn't made a peep. Nothing this morning, either, during my short and horrible Phoebe bathroom encounter. My theory was Phoebe overload.

"I think Phoebe killed it," I told Izzy when I finally got down to the basement after Dad and Claire left for work, and Gladys and Calvin were watching *Sesame Street.* "It couldn't take the stress. Or I squashed it lying on it. I hope it's not defunct."

I'd found him in a corner of the basement, sweeping. "The joint is jumping today," he said, nodding toward the laundry room. "Dirty napkins and tablecloths like you wouldn't believe. I've scouted out a more hospitable retreat. In fact, it's where I spent the night."

He put down the broom, and we walked toward the far end of the basement, into a room filled with rolled-up rugs, worn-out sofas, tables, old saggy armchairs. "Be it ever so humble," he said, climbing over a pile of mattresses, "there's no place like home." He pushed aside a broken-down crib, moved a pot of plastic sunflowers, and stretched out on a couch that had clearly belonged to someone with a lot of cats.

I pulled a red velvet chair next to him. A cloud of dust puffed out when I sat on it. I sneezed. Then I handed him the irkostat. I didn't really believe it was defunct. But saying that was easier than saying I'd let him down. "I hope it's still okay."

"Of course it's okay," he said as he pressed buttons. "It might need a bit of tweaking, if you'll pardon an annoying expression—"

Bzzzzzzzzzzzzzzzzzzzzzt!

He grinned. "See that? It just detected that delightful bag of goodies in your satchel." He reached over, unzipped my backpack, and took out the bag of food I'd brought for him. "Ah, yes. Candy canes, cookies, a partial chocolate Santa, some turkey—a mite rare, but most welcome. Yes, indeedy! Peckish doesn't begin to describe . . ." He bit off the Santa's shoe. "*Wunderbar!* Solid chocolate. I find the hollow Santas annoyingly depressing. You're not eating?"

I shook my head. I was glad he was feeling cheerful, but I wasn't sure why.

"So, no overnight revelations about the irkostat?" he said through a mouthful of turkey. "No breakthroughs, not a hint of a hint?"

"Not really." I told him what had happened. "When Phoebe was around, I couldn't shut it up. It was like it was in overdrive. Hyperdetect. Something. It did things I never saw it do before." I told him about the smell.

His eyes brightened. "This isn't bad, Lucas. It's good. It has to be. There is something extremely interesting going on. My sense is it involves intelligence. Yours."

"Mine?" He couldn't be saying I was brilliant again. I hadn't done anything.

"Indubitably." He sat up. "We're talking the power of creative outrage here. The only problem is finding out how to harness it."

"And we have to find out before I go home. It's Thursday, you know, Izzy. I've only got two more days—"

"Home? Two more days? What are you talking about?" He put down the Santa. "You're home."

"No." I couldn't believe he didn't know. "I'm here for vacation."

He didn't say anything.

"You didn't know that?"

"No, I didn't know that! How would I know that?"

"You know everything else about me."

He'd stopped looking confused and started looking angry. Really angry. "Oh, yes, the stupid gizmo detects every other stupid piece of information. It stinks out your sister, which no one asked it to do. It's been set to Detect this entire week, but the one thing I need it to do . . . the one vital . . . this irkostat is more than flaky, Lucas. It's useless." I thought he was going to throw it across the room. "So, where you going?"

"Connecticut." I couldn't look at him. "I live in Connecticut. Phoebe's my stepsister." I felt like I'd done something wrong. Way worse than letting him think I could fix the irkostat. And I hadn't told him yet that I was going downtown to meet Dad. "My mom went to the Bahamas. That's why I came here. I'm leaving Sunday morning."

I don't know if it was Izzy's face, when I finally did look up, or hearing myself say "leaving" that got to me. I couldn't believe I hadn't thought about leaving till now. I mean, I'd thought of it. When I was with Phoebe, I thought of nothing else, but when I was with Izzy, I was just with Izzy, and it felt like it would go on that way.

"Well, then"—he stuffed the food back in its bag, shoved it in my backpack, zipped the zipper, and jumped up—"let's get cracking. I see you've got your jacket. Let's head out." His voice was brisk, all business.

"You're mad at me now, right?" I said as he opened the door. I was glad he'd stopped looking at me. He was sorry he'd chosen me. I could tell. "I'm deserting you. I know. I'm sorry. I shouldn't have said I'd try to fix the irkostat. I'm really sorry."

"What are you talking about?" He turned. He was still scowling and his voice was gruff, but there was something else behind it. "Hey. Izzy Gribitz is an optimist. If I weren't, I'd have picked another line of work. And unless I'm totally mistaken, so would you."

The law firm where Dad worked was heavy duty: wood walls, paintings in carved gold frames, law magazines, *Investors Business Daily*, the *Wall Street Journal*. Even the flowers looked serious. "Hoo-hah! Fancy schmancy! Stodgo-rama!" I could imagine Izzy saying. "I'll take the passages anytime."

I wished Izzy could have come with me. He'd have walked up to the receptionist, looked her in the eye, and said, "Hey there, toots! What's new and exciting in your world?"

"He'll just be a minute, sweetheart," the receptionist said after I'd told her who I was and she'd buzzed Dad. "He's on a call. He'll be right out."

"That's fine. Thanks." Behind the glass doors I could see men bustling around in white shirts and ties, and women in Claire-type clothes. No wonder Dad and Claire took everything so seriously. I'd just cleared my throat for the third time and wiped my palms on my pants in case I needed to shake hands, and was trying to decide whether to keep my jacket on or take it off, sit or stay standing, when Dad came out.

"How'd the trip down go? You have any problem finding us?" He shook my hand. "Evidently not. You're here." His laugh seemed louder than at home. He seemed bigger, too. "Gloria, meet my son Lucas," he told the receptionist.

"Pleased to meet you," I said as she shook my hand.

He was doing Hearty Office Dad. I was Well-Brought-Up Office Visitor Lucas.

"This is my son," he told everyone as he led me down a carpeted hallway to his office. "Wow, you never told me you had such a grown-up son, Charles," they said. "So, Luke, how you enjoying the Big Apple?" "You going to be a lawyer like your dad?"

Well-Brought-Up Lucas shook everyone's hand and smiled and said, "Pleased to meet you." But I kept picturing Izzy staring back at that bow tie man, glaring at the lady who gawked at me around the side of her cubicle, and saying, "Now, 'cubicle,' that is a ridiculously irritating word. Lucas, you're not seriously going to let somebody who spends the day in a 'cubicle' make you nervous? Remember, the best defense is a good offense. Check it out: 'Think you could stare a little harder, buddy boy?' 'Pardon me, sir, is your face hurting you? Because it's killing me.' 'It's been a treat, poopsie. Gotta hop.'"

"Well, Lucas, hungry?" Dad said after I'd shaken hands with what felt like several thousand people and forgotten all their names, and he'd shown me his office and we'd waved to Claire, who was on her phone. "What do you say we find ourselves something to eat? There's a coffee shop I like over on Forty-eighth. That sound okay?"

"Yeah, I'm feeling a mite peckish," I said.

He looked at me like, *I beg your pardon?* But he didn't say anything.

"So your subway ride went okay?" he said again as we walked along the crowded street. "Any problems getting down?"

"No, it was fine." It was exciting being downtown, but it was weird that Dad and I kept having this same conversation. "It was easy," I said. "I like the subway."

If you didn't count that I couldn't get my MetroCard to work, and that the people lined up behind me at the turnstile weren't too happy when I stood there for five minutes while Izzy, off in a corner of the subway station, kept trying to get the irkostat's Correct function to let me through.

Dad looked like he was waiting for me to say more, so I added, "Your map was great," even though I hadn't needed it at all. I'd been here before, with Mom, when I was little, so I'd recognized his building. It still felt like the biggest one on Park Avenue. The lobby had mirrors everywhere and guard guys in blue uniforms and elevators that looked like they were made of gold and designed for giants. The Christmas ornaments hanging from the ceiling were so immense that if they fell on you, they'd squash you flat.

"This is a very popular place at lunch," Dad said when we got to the coffee shop.

"It's nice," I said. It was a million times spiffier than the bureau coffee shop. The waitress was nothing like Mabel. But many of the people in the booths looked like plainclothes Annoyance Bureau agents. It was amazing how many people on the subway looked like agents too.

"How's your burger?" Dad said when it arrived. "They're usually very good."

"Good. How's yours?"

"Very good." He looked at my already-empty glass. "You need another Coke?"

"No, thanks. I'm fine."

Hearty Office Dad and Office Visitor Lucas were running out of things to say.

And this burger wasn't as good as the ostrich burger. I wondered if I'd ever get to have another one. I wondered if Izzy would ever have another one.

"Dad, did you ever eat an ostrich burger?" I said.

"Can't say as I have," he said. "Have you?"

"Yeah. They're good."

"I'll take your word for it."

"I was just wondering if they had them here."

We both studied the menu.

"Nope. All I see is the old standard, high-cholesterol variety," he said. "Which is fine with me."

I wondered how long this lunch was going to last. Izzy'd said I should meet him in the furniture room when I got back. I wished I had a way to call him. It would be nice if the irkostat had a Phone function. Then, after Sunday, when I was back at home . . . no. I wasn't going to think about that.

"You know, Son, I don't know if I've told you," Dad was saying. "Claire and I really appreciate your getting along so well with everyone. You know, being so flexible, rolling with the punches. It takes all kinds, Lucas, as I'm sure you'll discover. Some are easier to get along with than others, but it's an important life skill, getting along with people of different types and genders and different personalities." He stopped to clear his throat. "And this is a tricky situation in certain ways. Situations like this can get a little tricky. And of course, we've had several other transitions of a somewhat major sort. . . ."

He kept picking up his coffee cup to see if there was anything still in it. He kept clearing his throat. Was he talking about me, or Phoebe?

"There've been a few times I was tempted to ask Claire if she thought I should be more proactive, and then I thought, *No, Lucas is doing well. Lucas seems to be having a fine time,* and besides"—there was the Hearty Office Dad laugh again—"you know women. You get them involved and they tend to magnify things out of all proportion. And besides, I'd say that all of the aforementioned things you seem to be handling. Do you agree? You seem to be managing them very well."

"Proactive," there's another one for your list! That's what Izzy would say. Not to mention "aforementioned"!

"Thanks," answered Office Visitor Lucas.

Izzy would go ballistic if he heard me say that. *"Thanks"? That's it? You're done? It's slipped your mind what that pestiferous potato told you this morning?* Which was that she thought I'd want to know that the only reason Alex seemed so interested in me was that Alex had to write a three-hundred-word personal essay about her strangest relative. I should have told Phoebe strange was better than vicious. I should have told her a lot more than that.

136

"Not totally," I added.

"You don't totally agree?" Dad said. "Or you're not totally handling it? Sorry." He checked his coffee cup again. "Claire hates when I do that. Claire's always been better at this sort of thing than I. Your mom, too, for that matter. Women are generally in charge of the relationship aspects of relationships. You'd think a lawyer would be better at words, wouldn't you? You'd think this would be easier."

"Dad?" It would be easier if I knew whether he was talking about him and me, or him and Phoebe, or me and Phoebe. He might not even know Phoebe was vicious and quite possibly a liar. Not "possibly," indubitably, I could hear Izzy saying. Dad might not know Phoebe was so sneaky. "Dad, you're good at fixing things, right?" Why was I bringing that up now? "Dad, you're, like, engineerically inclined."

"Hardly." He made a face. "By the way, are we still talking about relationships?"

"Not necessarily." Maybe that's why I'd brought it up. Because he'd stopped being Hearty Office Dad and had gone back to being Alone with Lucas Dad, which made me even more uncomfortable. "I was just thinking of the stuff we used to build. Those LEGO constructions, remember? And those fortresses we made for the Transformers? With the blocks and everything?"

"They were really something," he said.

Yeah, it was good I'd changed the subject. And they were really something. They had covered my whole floor. "Dad, remember that Autobot fortress?" Everything we made had to be a fortress, or Aslan would step in it or bash it over with his tail.

Dad smiled. "Ah yes, Computron. Technobot, Super Warrior. Strength: nine point zero. Intelligence: ten point zero. Speed: two point zero. Skill: nine point zero. Et cetera, et cetera . . ."

"How do you remember that?" I said. "Even I don't remember his specs."

"You made me read tech specs to you every night," he said. "And you always made me say the 'point zero.'"

I laughed. "That must have been annoying."

"Not to you," he said. "And not as annoying as trying to remember which guy was which. Nosecone, Slash, Sludge, Grudge—"

"There was no Grudge." I could feel my throat relaxing.

"Was it the Dinobot fortress that Aslan lay down in?" Dad was starting to look more normal too.

"Uh-uh." The Dinobot fortress was what we'd built right before Dad moved out. I left it up until Mom said the dust balls were going to roll out of my room and take over the world. "It was the LEGO space station. And it was so cool building that, remember? We worked so hard. We did such a perfect job."

"It was cool, wasn't it?" Dad said. "But I hate to tell you. You were always way better at building than I was."

"I was?"

"Yes. I basically sat there and you'd say, 'Hey, Dad, pass me the whatever,' and I'd pass it, and you'd build it."

I looked at him. "Really? I remember that we did all of it together."

"The way I remember it, I'd do something and you'd go, 'No, Dad, not that one, Dad. Dad, that's all wrong. Dad, you're not too good at this.' And don't let me try to transform your Transformers. . . ."

"Oh, right." I laughed. I hadn't thought about this in so long. "I really was somewhat annoying, wasn't I? More than somewhat."

"I wouldn't say that." He stopped to think about it. "Well, maybe, but in a good way, if you know what I mean."

I nodded.

"We always had a good time, you and I. . . ."

"Yeah," I said. "That was so much fun. It'll be fun when Calvin's old enough to build fortresses."

"I might need you to do it with us," he said.

"Okay," I said. "Yeah. I can do that. I can bring him some LEGO blocks. And some of the Transformers—"

"In which case, you'll definitely have to help him," Dad said. "Because I have not gotten better at this over time. I probably won't even be able to read the tech specs, never mind figure out what twists how and what unsnaps where. . . . You know that ride-on thing we gave him? Looks like it'd be simple to assemble, right? You probably could have put it together in five minutes. Instead of pulling my hair out, I should have waited for you to get here."

"You could have," I said.

"Next time I will. Speaking of pulling my hair out"—he laughed—"I could have used you at four thirty in the morning last week. I don't know if I told you. We were lying there fast asleep, it's the middle of the night, and something starts chirping. Really loud. First I thought it was the alarm clock. Then I check to see if it's my watch, which I still haven't mastered. Then I check the baby monitor, which incidentally, I could use some help programming too. And it's still chirping, and Claire is going, 'Charles! Charles, I can't sleep. Charles, you have to make it stop! It's going to wake Calvin.' And I'm thinking, *Never mind Calvin. Please just don't let it wake Phoebe!*"

So then he *was* talking about Phoebe before. He didn't want to come out and say so, but he agreed with me. "So, what was it? It sounds like a battery running out—"

"That's absolutely correct! It was the smoke alarm, and I couldn't get it to stop. I thought, *I am either going to have to hit it with a hammer or throw it out the window.*"

"So did you take the battery out?" I said, wondering if I dared say something about Phoebe now.

"Eventually." He made a face. "So, the answer to 'Are you engineerically inclined?' is, I don't think so. Next time something's not working right, I'm calling you."

I was already somewhat happy, but as Dad called for the check and then walked me to the subway, this weird, amazing cheerfulness came over me. Not just because he'd told me I was good at things, or because he said he wanted me to come back. It was great knowing I wasn't the only one who couldn't deal with Phoebe, knowing it would take a miracle to deal with Phoebe, knowing even my dad thought she was the big potato. Which made me what? Optimistically pessimistic? Like good in an annoying sort of way? Or would it be pessimistically optimistic, like annoying in a good way? Or vice versa. Izzy would know. I couldn't wait to ask him.

CHAPTER 18

"Out on annoyance patrol. Working on your lists."

Izzy's note was on the velvet chair in the furniture room.

This wasn't good. I'd seen too many green-coat guys on my way back from the subway, heard his name muttered into walkie-talkies too many times. Then there were the flyers I'd spotted in a trash can, with the same mug shot as the flyer Hildegund had shown me and a hot-line number to call and all sorts of stupid stuff about Izzy being an aggravated nuisance. I'd brought one to show him, thinking we'd laugh about it. Now I wondered if it was Izzy who'd crunched them up and thrown them in the trash.

The laundry room was empty except for a lady putting her clothes in the dryer.

"Do you have change for a dollar?" I asked her. She did. I went to the pay phone and left Dad a message that I was back safely. Then I called Gladys and promised her I'd be home before it got dark.

Where would Izzy have gone? If he was working on my lists, then not to Book World. My lists had nothing book-related on them. Most of my annoyances had to do with Phoebe. It'd be great if he were working on Phoebe. But I doubted he could do anything without the Correct function. His extranatural snap-your-fingers-and-it-vanishes powers couldn't make people disappear—only things. It couldn't even move people to a distribution depot. Which left the squirt gun. Which I had no objection to. But he'd never risk going to the apartment and seeing Gladys.

I was about to take the elevator to the lobby when I noticed the brown fingerprints on the door to the passages. I walked over and, trying to look as if I always went around smelling doors, took a sniff. It smelled like chocolate.

This really wasn't good. It was the day after Christmas. The passages had to be crawling with agents. They probably all had the flyers. It worried me how fast the bureau had gotten those flyers out. It meant they weren't the doofuses Izzy thought. Not when they were against you.

My haircut wasn't much of a disguise. I wished I had my hat. But I didn't, so I did the only thing I could think of. I went back to the furniture room, tore a blank ABGNY Post-it from the pad Izzy'd left his note on, and wrote myself a pass. Then, since passes always had signatures, and the only Higher-up I knew was Hildegund, I signed her name. Then I waited till the lady in the laundry room left, and wedged the Post-it pad in the door so I couldn't get locked out.

Lucas Graham might not be brilliant, but he was not dumb. And he was trying.

Which way to go, though? Which way would Izzy go? Not toward New Jersey. I started walking east. The passages didn't smell like onions today. They smelled like some kind of perfume. I'd only walked a short way when I saw an overturned cart with broken perfume bottles all around and one of the cart guys cursing.

I was right about the day after Christmas. The passages were full of carts. At first I glanced up only long enough to look for Izzy and keep my bearings. But the guys trudging or driving by seemed too stressed and grumpy to bother with me, so I started checking out their carts. Most seemed to be full of broken toys, but I also spotted those beeping, blinking Christmas tree lights; some very wide ties; some very narrow ties; crazy shoes with six-inch heels. Why remote-control vehicles, though? Kids loved them. And why Transformers? Izzy was right. These Annoyance Bureau types had no clue.

Then I noticed the wheelbarrow full of raisins and the cart piled with hamster wheels—both items from my lists. A cart filled with Bubble Yum went by, and a wagonload of glitter. And birdcall clocks? This had to be Izzy! I just hoped he hadn't gotten that cartload of knock-knock joke books from Book World. Barber impersonation was one thing. But impersonating an Annoyance Bureau agent? At Book World? That scared me.

I pulled out my pass and flagged down a guy driving a golf cart. "Excuse me!" I had to shout over the racket from the musical Christmas cards he was moving. I had a horrible feeling I'd seen them in Book World too. He pulled over. "Do you happen to know somebody named Izzy Gribitz?"

"Why? You a friend of his?" I couldn't see his eyes behind the dark glasses, but I didn't like the way his voice sounded.

"Me? No. I don't even know him. I just . . . you know, saw the flyers. . . ."

"What, you're after the reward money?"

"There's a reward? For Izzy?"

Uh-oh. Now he'd know I knew him.

"There's an APB out," he said. "The whole bureau's looking for him. It just came over the radio."

"What'd he do?"

"Stepped on the wrong toes. Stuck his nose where it had no business." He let out a laugh. "Lemme tell ya. The boys in the Division of Horn Honking are pretty steamed."

I didn't think I smiled, but he took off his reflector glasses and looked me over. "That wouldn't be what you're doing, would it? Nosing around?" He stared at my nose.

Or was it my hair? "Wait! You're that kid from the coffee shop. You were with him! And didn't I see you in Book World one time, when I was making a pickup?"

"No"—I shook my head—"that wasn't me."

"Yeah, it was. What are you doin' down here?"

A wheelbarrow passed by loaded with *Overcoming the Annoying Habits That Wreck Homes and Destroy Your Peace of Mind*, and then a cart filled with *Annoying Habits Can Be Overcome*. The books Izzy had confiscated and Agent Pellet had put back. He *had* gone to Book World.

Now I was really scared.

"Hey. You don't answer when people talk to you? I asked what you're doing down here."

I showed him my pass. It didn't seem nearly as smart now as when I'd written it.

He looked it over, scowled, shook his head, did one of those horse snorts, and shook his head again. "You're as bad as my kid! Man, you're lucky you stopped me and not one of the other guys!" He nodded toward the carts going by in both directions. "If you'd stopped one of them and shown them this? Forget it. They'd be packing you off to HQ as we speak." He crumpled the Post-it. "Where'd you pick this bureau pad up, anyway? How'd you get down?" He leaned over the side of his cart and peered around. So did I. "You're not with Gribitz now, are you? What's your name?"

I said the first name that popped into my head. "Calvin."

"Okay, Cal. Because I'm a nice guy, I'm gonna give you a ride home. Right now."

"No, thanks. That's okay." I had to find Izzy. "I'll walk."

"You'll ride," he said. "Hop on. Anyone asks, I'll say I caught you down here and I'm taking you to HQ. Sing out when you see your door. Then you go up and you stay up. You do not poke your nose into bureau business. And you realize if we run into Gribitz, I've gotta take him in."

When we got back to my door, the cart guy held it open, stood at the bottom of the stairs, and watched till I was all the way up. "And you stay away from Gribitz, if you know what's good for you!" he warned.

I'd been worrying that someone would remove the ABGNY Post-it pad from the laundry room door. It was still wedged in tight. I checked to make sure the place was empty. Then I ran to the furniture room. Maybe Izzy was there now. Maybe I'd been worried about nothing. Maybe he was waiting for me.

He wasn't.

CHAPTER 19

I sneaked out of the apartment several times that night to check the basement, and the minute I woke up Friday morning I checked again. If Izzy had been back, he'd left me no sign.

I had to find him. I didn't dare try the passages again. I didn't know where else to look except Book World, so as soon as Dad and Claire went to work, I headed out.

The street outside the store was swarming with agents. I could see them from a block away. I could hear the crackle of their walkie-talkies.

"Hot spot at Book World. Copy."

"Confiscation on schedule. Do you read me? Over."

"Rogue agent removal action in process. Roger."

I'd started running the instant the idea popped into my head. It looked like I was too late.

Gladys had thought I was crazy going out in the freezing rain. She wouldn't let me out the door without the tassel hat. I'd wondered, as I started over, if Correct could have made the rain stop. Or made the streets less icy. Not that it mattered without the irkostat. Without Izzy. It probably couldn't have anyway. "We're not on Cybertron," he'd said that time

I thought he was going to transform into a robot. Or turn me into one. No, the Annoyance Bureau only dealt with small stuff.

I was slipping and sliding toward Broadway, thinking how long ago that seemed, wishing Izzy *could* have transformed me—given me some better tech specs: more intelligence, more power, more speed—when I heard *Beep! Beep! Beep! Beep!* First I was sure it was the irkostat. But it was only a car alarm. Izzy might have banished honking horns . . . *Beep! Beep! Beep! Beep!* That had to be a ten on the Gribitz scale. Somebody should take out the battery, like Dad did with the smoke alarm. Or bash it with a hammer.

Which is what got me thinking. What if the irkostat had a battery, and the battery had gone bad? The irkostat looked as if it didn't open. But I knew it did. I'd seen that hatch where Izzy got the scissors. That might have been Izzy's powers; he'd said he'd given it a mental message. Or the irkostat could be like a Transformer. Which only transformed when you knew how.

This wasn't a breakthrough; it was barely a hint of a hint. Even if I was right, it wasn't as if I had a backpack full of batteries. But that's why I'd been running.

There weren't only guys in green coats outside Book World. There were guys in green suits with gold braid and brass buttons. That had to be the Higher-ups.

Hildegund had on a green suit today too. "Grabitz to Repository," I heard her say into her walkie-talkie. "Prepare for delivery. Over. Coming through! Step aside, Agents!"

Repository? Oh, no. And she'd gotten her name back?

I followed her into the store and over to the escalator, then got on behind her. There seemed to be more agents than customers today. "You won't see me shedding any tears. It's been a long time coming!" I heard her say into her walkie-talkie as the escalator took us to the top floor. I followed her to the far corner and threaded my way through the crowd of agents, trying to see what they were gawking at.

I'd known it was Izzy. I'd known from the minute I got there. But this was worse than I had dreamed. He was tied to a hand truck with bungee cords, like that squawking scarecrow we'd seen being carted off to the Repository. He couldn't even squawk. His mouth was covered with duct tape. His eyes were open, but his face looked blank, like he was in a trance or had given up.

I don't know how long I stood there, not breathing, not swallowing, my brain frozen, watching as a big, hulking agent grabbed the handles of the hand truck, tipped it back, and started wheeling Izzy toward the elevator—the elevator to the passages.

Then I realized. If I moved to the other side of that table right there, he couldn't get to the elevator without passing me.

I had to get Izzy's attention. I tried a mental message. He didn't look up.

I climbed onto the table and started waving my arms.

"Irk!" I said.

Nothing.

"Irk!" I squawked it. "*Irk! Irk!*" I flapped my arms. Maybe the Higher-ups would take me for some nut who thought he was a bird. "*IRK!*" *Please. Let Izzy see me!*

He saw me then. His eyes brightened slightly.

They'd bungee-corded him around his legs and shoulders. Could he get his hand into his pocket? Did he even have the irkostat? And if he had it and passed it to me, could I do anything? I had no idea. All I knew was I couldn't stand here watching while my friend got carted off to the final resting place for the worst of the worst.

"IRK!" He was only a few feet away from me now. I'd been doing a basic arms-out bird flap. Now I brought them forward and flapped lower, pointing my index fingers toward his pockets. *"IRRRK!" Get it, Izzy? Please. Get it.*

He got it.

But now Hildegund was pointing at me. "Would somebody kindly do something about that idiot in the appalling hat?"

She didn't recognize me. Which gave me courage. I jumped down. Izzy was slowly easing his hand into his pocket. I edged closer to him. And closer. And as the hand truck passed by he slipped the irkostat into the pocket of my jacket.

Now I was positive it opened. I just had to figure out how, and without anyone seeing it. I ducked behind a bookcase. If it were a Transformer, how would it transform? I wasn't sure opening it would do any good, but I ran my fingers over it, feeling for seams, gaps, anything. I pressed everywhere. There had to be a hatch. It had to be in the bottom. I pressed; I wiggled, looking for the tiniest movement, the smallest play, a little give, a place where I could twist.

And there it was.

"And it's about time!" I heard Hildegund say. I looked up. The hand truck was almost at the elevator door. *Please let the elevator not be here! Let it be down in the passages!*

· Keeping one eye on the hand truck, I opened the hatch. I was right. It had a battery. Not only that, the battery looked like it was in backward. I took it out, put it in the other way, and closed the hatch.

The screen lit up.

Had I fixed it? Did I dare hope? The buttons still had no labels. I pressed one. HIGH appeared on the screen. Excellent!

I pressed another. INSPECT. Great! DEFROST? CALCULATOR? What was this? UNDO, CLOCK RADIO, MEMORY, FAST-FORWARD, DETECT, MUTE, BROIL, LIQUEFY, PEDOMETER, PERMANENT PRESS? Where was CORRECT? Was this some horrible joke?

Maybe not.

It had an EJECT button.

The hand-truck guy was pressing the elevator button. The door was opening.

I pressed EJECT. The bungee cords burst open. Izzy shot into the air like a rocket. He was gone.

The agents were almost as stunned as I was.

"What? What happened? How'd he do that? Where'd Gribitz go?"

"It's a miracle!"

"It must have been that device of his!"

"Gotta be the device."

"What? You're kidding! You mean that thing works?"

Some of the Higher-ups looked furious. Others just seemed amazed. A few looked impressed.

Uh-oh. Agent Zapp had spotted me. He was pointing me out to Hildegund.

I was pretty sure I remembered which the Detect button was. I had no idea if you could press two at once, or if it could find Izzy. I pushed Detect, Eject.

Next thing I knew, I was standing on Broadway, across the street from Book World. Next to Izzy.

"Brilliant!" He slapped me on the back, pounded my shoulder, threw his arms around me. "That was brilliant! You're brilliant. You feel okay?"

"Yeah!" I couldn't stop laughing. "What about you?" He looked fine. Except for his toupee and mustache, which must have blown off.

"It's not my preferred mode of travel," he said, dusting his jacket, "but hey, I'm outta there, you're outta there, and you fixed the irkostat!"

"Why do you think that engineer put on all those crazy buttons?" I said. "I mean, I can understand the functions and the Mute button and Undo—"

"I don't know and I don't care!" He was pounding me again. "I love that engineer! Can you imagine Izzy Gribitz locked in the Repository with the most annoying annoyances of all time? He saved me from a fate worse than . . ." He raised his finger in the air. "Correction! It wasn't the engineer at all. It was you!"

He took out a handkerchief and wiped his neck. It was raining even harder now. The street was even icier. "Whooh! I'd give anything to have seen Hildegund's face when I blasted off. All those obnoxiously officious, interfering Higher—"

"Izzy?" We'd been so busy congratulating ourselves we'd forgotten the agents. I looked across at Book World. No one was coming out. "Izzy, where are they? What are they doing?"

"I don't know. You're the man with the irkostat. What'd you press?"

"No clue. Could have been anything. Let me see." I took it out of my pocket and started to press buttons.

"Whoa! Whoa! Not so fast on the trigger. This baby is powerful. Hold down Off while you press. It'll neutralize any mental messages." He pointed to a button on the bottom row.

"Okay." I held it down, pressed buttons, and read their functions off the screen. "Help, Menu, Frappé, Redial, Select, Direct—so there aren't only four -ects!" I *was* brilliant. I turned it over. "Spray/Mist? Cold? What'd this guy do, use old buttons off anything he could find? Rewind, Snooze—"

"Snooze! Bingo. There's your answer." Izzy shook my hand. "They're asleep!"

This was so awesome! "Where's Correct, though?"

"Right here." He took the irkostat from me. "I knew where it was, Lucas. I just couldn't make it work. I'm assuming it works now. Shall we give it a try?"

"Yeah, but not here!" I was still expecting hordes of enraged agents to storm out of Book World. "If that Snooze button's from an alarm clock, we've only got ten minutes."

"So press it again."

"Won't it make us fall asleep?"

His finger went up again. "That's where the mental messages come in. Remember. This baby is a hunk of junk without the mental messages."

"So, what shall we correct?" he said as we walked down Broadway.

"Can we stop this pestiferous rain?" It couldn't hurt to ask.

He shook his head, as I'd expected. "Out of my league, Lucas. Annoyances, that's our department. The everyday stuff, that's what we fix. By which I do not mean small stuff. As you well know, when you're annoyed, there is no small stuff. Which is where we come in." He pointed to an icy patch on the sidewalk. "Press CORRECT, then LIQUEFY."

I did. The ice melted.

"And HIGH, HOT, CORRECT might help your sneakers. It would probably do a fine job drying those pants, too."

It did.

"Izzy," I said. "Do you think the engineer got the cat whirler knob off a washing machine? You know, spin cycle?"

"We'll never know." He held out his hand. "Let me see that thing a minute."

I handed him the irkostat. He pointed it at a heap of discarded Christmas trees lying on the curb outside an apartment building. "I've always found cast-off Christmas trees profoundly annoying. Don't you agree?"

"They're sad," I said.

"That's what I mean," he said. "One day they're glittering and gorgeous, the next they're lying naked and abandoned in the gutter. Shall we do something about it?"

Before I'd answered, the trees were in the center island of Broadway. Standing up. A miniature forest.

"Wow!" I said.

"You bet your bippy. How do you feel about potholes?"

"I don't like them," I said.

"I agree." He pointed the irkostat at a big, gaping one. It paved itself over.

By lunchtime we'd filled the center island of Broadway with Christmas trees. The rain, freezing on their needles, sparkled like diamonds.

We fixed broken pay phones up and down Broadway. We corrected people's blown-out umbrellas, halted curbside splashes before they happened, kept some lady from smacking her kid, stopped the pepperoni from sliding off my pizza, and changed Broadway from Grocery-Cart Road Rage Central to Pleasantville.

We stayed out all morning and all afternoon, making sure to press Snooze every few minutes. We didn't see a single agent.

"Whooh! I'm pooped!" Izzy said finally. "We've taken care of most of the items on your lists. This old dog needs a nap. Let's head home. My feet are killing me."

"Can't you just correct that?" I said. I dreaded going back. I'd tried all day not to think about it. Phoebe was having a slumber party. I didn't have just one big, pestiferously pestilential potato to deal with. There'd be four of them.

And then I remembered.

Izzy stopped walking. "What's funny? Tell me. I like to laugh."

"Izzy?" I said. "You think I can keep the irkostat with me tonight? You won't be needing it, right? You don't need to correct anything in the basement."

I might not be ready for the pestilential-potato party, but the irkostat would be.

The party was going strong when I got back. I could hear the music through my wall.

I opened the bathroom door. The girls stopped dancing. Phoebe's eyebrow went up. "I didn't hear you knock," she said.

I patted my pocket to make sure the irkostat was still there. "I didn't."

Somebody paused the music. Phoebe folded her arms, looking at me—waiting, I knew, for me either to leave or to say something they could laugh at. They were all looking at me. Why was that? I fought the urge to look in the mirror and see if my hair was sticking up.

No. Wrong. Not sticking up. Standing up.

"Do you think I could use your computer a minute?" I said from the bathroom. "I want to check my e-mail."

Phoebe's eyebrow rose higher. "And that would be because . . . ?" She looked over at her friends.

"Because I might have some e-mail?"

"This isn't an ideal time," she said.

Here's where I was supposed to back down and go away. Except I wanted to know if I had any e-mail.

"But you're going to say yes, right?" I said. "Because I've been here a week and I haven't asked you for a single thing." I stepped into her room—the first time since I'd been coming to this apartment. Her room made my room look like Neatness World. It didn't smell that good either. "Because you've been pushing me around, bossing me around, going"—I dropped my mouth open and imitated her slump-sigh—"or"—I put out my tongue and stuck my finger down my throat—"or raising your unspeakable eyebrow every time I say anything."

Phoebe's eyes were bulging. Her friends had started out making uh-oh faces at one another. Now they were looking more like, Hmmm. This is getting interesting.

Which made me keep going. "And because I've been persistently pleasant to you and your carbunculated cat, and put up with every ridiculously irritating thing you said, no matter how annoyingly preposterous or preposterously annoying"—one of them snickered; I wished I could remember more of the Gribitz scale—"and because I know you don't want your friends to see you acting like a rodential retread or to know what a pedunculated pissant you are, and that—"

"What did you just call her?" One of the girls, I think Zoë, had totally cracked up. "Pe-dunk-you-lated? What is pe-dunk-you-lated?"

"And what's a pissant?" Chloe was laughing too. I was pretty sure Chloe was the short one. "I've always wondered what a pissant—"

"It's a cut above a crapulent carbuncle." I could see why Izzy liked telling people off. I could see getting into this. I gave Phoebe the same annoying finger-flapping wave Izzy'd used on Hildegund. "Adieu, O crapulent carbuncle!"

I should have quit before the *adieu*. Even I knew *adieu* meant "good-bye." Now I probably had to leave.

I was about to exit through the bathroom when Zoe said, "Hey, Lucas. Where you going? I thought you wanted to check your e-mail."

"Oh. Right," I said.

"You don't have to go." She glanced over at Phoebe. "Right, Phebe? Lucas can stay."

"Yeah. Let him check his e-mail." That was Schmoe. I think her name was Sophie. "It's not like you're on the phone, O crapulent carbuncle."

"Shut up!"

I could hear Phoebe was trying to sound as if she was joking. But it was obvious to me she couldn't stand it. She couldn't stand that her friends thought I was funny. She couldn't stand that they didn't hate me. That they might like me. She couldn't stand that Calvin wanted to be with me and that Tinkerbell followed me around. That Claire really liked me. And that my dad was happy I was here.

It was driving her berserk.

I went over to her computer, sat down, and logged on.

She crowded in over my shoulder. "Looking for something from your special someone?"

"Excuse me. Would you mind?" I did a little *Back off!* wave thing with my hand.

I expected her to say, "Would I mind *what?*" But her eyebrow stayed down.

Not only that, she backed off.

This was as good as rescuing Izzy!

I downloaded my mail. There was something. From Alexandra: *"Hey. Whassup. Nada here. Boring and annoying. Kewl meeting u. Well, gtg."*

"You, too. NOT boring here!" I replied. *"BTW, do you know what a pedunculated pissant is? P.S. You can use this same e-mail address when I'm back at home."*

"I'm done," I said when I'd hit Send. "Thanks."

"You can stay if you want," Sophie said.

"Yeah, right, Phebe?" Chloe said.

I raised my eyebrow. "I don't think so." Then I left—through the hall door, not the bathroom.

It wasn't till I was in my room that I realized. I'd forgotten to use the irkostat. I hadn't even thought about it. Not once.

CHAPTER 20

I wasn't sure how I was going to get the irkostat back to Izzy the next morning. Dad and Claire had a whole day planned for us. Dad was making a special breakfast. Later we were going to the American Museum of Natural History, then to a movie, then out to dinner.

My last day before going home.

I slept late. Dad was working on the pancakes and Claire was squeezing the juice when I came in. I had never liked grapefruit juice before, but I was starting to.

"I just went down for the mail," she said, pouring me a glass. Then she handed me a postcard.

> *The beaches are fantastic here, but I can't*
> *wait to see you. Pick you up at the Fairfield*
> *station Sunday afternoon, as planned.*
> *XOXO*
> *Mom*

I wondered if she'd pick up Aslan at the kennel first, or if we'd go together.

"You know, I've gotten used to having you around," Claire said. "I'm going to miss you."

Dad nodded. "Me too. And I'm glad you'll get to do some fun things today, finally."

I looked at him. "Is Phoebe coming with us?"

"I kind of doubt it," Claire said. "I'm not sure when they'll wake up. They were up most of the night." I knew. I'd heard them through the wall. "I hope you don't mind."

"Oh, no, it's fine," I said. "Don't worry. I won't take it personally."

Tinkerbell still couldn't believe there wasn't something delicious for him in my pocket. He jumped on my lap and started sniffing around. Gladys scurried over, picked him up, and set him on the floor.

It was Saturday. Didn't this lady ever take a day off?

"You bad boy, Tinkie!" she scolded. "You leave Lukey Duke alone!"

"Gladys?" I said. "Do you think you could not call me Lukey Duke? Or Lukey? It's okay when you're three. I like being called Lucas."

Dad and Claire looked at each other but didn't say anything.

"Oh! Why, certainly, Lucas!" Gladys was shocked, but she recovered fast. She turned to Calvin in his high chair. "Calvin! From now on we call him Lucas! You'll help me remember that, won't you?" He woofed. "I don't know what you think, Calvin," she said, "but I think we should send your big brother, Lucas, home with clean clothes!"

I started to say how it was okay, how Mom wouldn't care at all, how we'd wash the clothes when I got home. Till I realized the laundry was my ticket to the basement. "I'll take it down right after breakfast," I said. "I'll take yours, too, if you want, Gladys."

"That's so nice! I've got a full bag!" She beamed at Claire. "Isn't Lucas nice?"

Izzy was in the furniture room crossing items off my lists when I got there.

"So, d'you give those buttons a workout last night?" he said when I handed him the irkostat. "Did you make a hash of the big potato? Did it do everything you wanted?"

I tried my best to look cool. "I didn't use it."

"What, she had a miraculous personality change? Her tongue fell out? She moved to Kathmandu?" He looked disappointed. "Don't tell me she wasn't home."

"She was home," I said. "I told her to back off."

His eyes widened. "And she did?"

I nodded. Then I grinned so wide I thought my face would crack.

"Whoo-hoo!" He pounded me on the arm and did a jig. "Why am I not surprised?" He stopped dancing and pointed his finger in the air. "This is an important life lesson, Lucas. Don't forget it. Inside every big potato is a Tater Tot."

"A teeny, tiny Tater Tot," I said. We started walking to the laundry room. "You know, you look better without the toupee and mustache," I said. "You look younger."

"I feel younger," he said. "Of course, I no longer have a hiding place for the irkostat. Not that I foresee needing one."

We had the laundry room to ourselves. I sorted the wash as Gladys had explained—lights in one machine, darks in another—poured in the Tide, put the quarters in the slots, and pushed in the slot thingies. "Our future is bright, my friend," he said as the machines started up. "The world is our oyster. The annoyers will tremble when they see us. The annoyed will cheer and breathe a sigh of—"

The passage door burst open. A man in a green suit with gold braid and brass buttons marched in. He was carrying a briefcase. Three more Higher-ups and many agents strode in after him. "So there you are!" he told Izzy.

"It's the Big Cheese!" Izzy whispered. "Let's get out of here!" He grabbed my arm. The agents crowded around us—Tuber, Zapp, Pellet, Bramble, and at least ten more. No Hildegund.

"What's your rush?" the Big Cheese said. "Surely you're not leaving? Not when it took so long to find you! And we never would have without Arthur, here." He nodded toward the golf cart guy from the other day, who gave me a salute.

"Heavens to Murgatroyd," Izzy whispered. "They're smiling!"

"Hey-hey! It's the man of the hour!" One of the agents clapped Izzy on the back.

"How's it goin', old buddy?" Another started shaking Izzy's hand.

"Grib, my man!" That couldn't be Elpidio Zapp with that big grin on his face!

"Gribby baby!" Was that Casimir Pellet?

All the agents were pumping his hand now. Patting him. One of the Higher-ups had a plastic shopping bag. He put it on the table and opened it. A delicious smell wafted out. "Care for an ostrich burger, Iz, old bean? We brought enough for everyone. Courtesy of Mabel, one of your many fans. She wished she could have been here. . . ."

"That was an extremely impressive demo you put on for us," the Big Cheese said as Izzy looked from one to another of the agents, shaking his head. "Marvelous! Simply marvelous! We're remarkably rested and refreshed, thanks to you." He stepped closer. "The bureau needs that device, Agent Gribitz."

Izzy caught my eye and eased closer to the table. "Better safe than sorry," he whispered, slipping the irkostat into Gladys's laundry bag. "I've been saying that to you for years," he told the Big Cheese.

"And we should have listened!" the Cheese answered. "That device is amazing. It's revolutionary. You'll patent it. We'll make more of them. We'll make hundreds. Thousands. What's it called again?"

"Irkostat." Izzy rolled his eyes at me.

"Great name!" Agent Zapp said.

"Love the name!" agreed Agent Tuber.

"Outstanding!" said Agent Pellet.

"Lucas thought of it," Izzy said.

"I'm impressed." The Cheese stuck his lower lip out and looked me over, nodding. "This is exactly what I'm getting at, Gribitz. Fresh blood. New ideas. Your irkostat can transform our operation. We're ripe for transformation—"

"Overripe," Izzy said. "Rotten."

"Rancid," I added.

Izzy looked surprised, but only for a second.

The Cheese was still talking. "We see an irkostat in every agent's pocket. First in the district, then the region, and then . . . who knows?"

"How would that work?" I looked at Izzy.

"We'll have to see about that," Izzy told the Cheese.

"I can see why you'd be cautious," the Cheese said. "Possibly even suspicious. But it's not only the device we're after, Gribitz. We want you. We need you back. Choose your venue. Maybe you're sick of New York City. Maybe it's time for greener pastures. And we're not talking Lapland, Special Agent. You'll pardon me for presuming to call you Special Agent. I can't help but think of you that way. Possibly even Chief—"

"This is the most egregious sucking up I've ever encountered," Izzy whispered to me. "I don't know about you, Lucas, but I'm nauseous."

"I think it's great!" I said. "I think it's about time."

"I'm not a free agent anymore," he told the Cheese. "My partner was the one who got the irkostat fully operational. I may have invented it, but Lucas ironed out the kinks." He put his arm around me. "So when you're talking to me, you're also talking to Lucas."

"Discuss it with Lucas, then," the Cheese said. "We're not talking instant decision. Think about it. Consider the offers. These are a small sampling of what's come in on the fax. There are e-mails, too. Dozens." He emptied the briefcase onto the table. It was a humongous pile. "Let's go, Agents. Let's give Special Agent Gribitz and his partner time to mull. Gentlemen, enjoy your ostrich burgers. We'll be in touch."

"They want you!" I shouted the instant they had gone. "They love you! '*Mah*-velous! Simply *mah*-velous!'"—I did my Big Cheese imitation—"'You're the best, babe! You're the man! Enjoy your ostrich burgers, old bean!'"

Izzy was still shaking his head, but he'd started giggling. He began flipping through the pile of papers. "E-mails, faxes, phone messages! Patagonia! Paramus! Princeton! The mind boggles—"

"Albany, Athens, Auckland . . ." I was looking through them too. "They're from bookstores, Izzy!"

"Of course they're from bookstores, Lucas! I'm a bookish kind of guy."

"Chain bookstores, regular bookstores, kids' bookstores, even a sci-fi bookstore. Biloxi, Copenhagen, Edinburgh, Fossil Falls . . . Izzy!" I shouted. "There's one here from Connecticut! Izzy, it's from Fairfield! That's right where I live!"

CHAPTER
21

I was glad they took me to the train the next morning. Grand Central Station was so big. There were so many people. We bought my ticket from a ticket guy I could have sworn worked for the bureau. Then Dad and Claire helped me find the track and walked me down the ramp to the train.

I was actually a little sad to be leaving them. I wasn't sad that Phoebe didn't come.

"Bye-bye!" Calvin called, waving from his stroller.

"Charles!" Claire grabbed Dad's arm. "Charles, did you hear that? Calvin said 'bye-bye'! He said his first word!"

"His big brother seems to have inspired him." Dad scooped Calvin from the stroller, pulled me to him, and hugged us both.

"Calvin sandwich!" I said, which was what Mom and Dad had always said when I was little and I was the one in the middle. I gave the tassel on his hat a yank.

He giggled and pulled the tassel on mine. "Bye-bye, Yukas!" he said, like it was no biggie, like he'd been talking for years, or could have if he'd felt the urge.

"*Hasta la* bye-bye, Calvin," I said. "See you soon."

"Yukas!" He looked over Dad's shoulder and waved. "Bye-bye, Izzy!"

"What'd he say?" Claire asked. "I didn't catch that."

"Izzy!" Calvin said again. "Yukas! Izzy!"

I broke from the hug. Izzy, right on schedule and carrying his coat, was trotting down the ramp toward the train.

He lagged behind, though, until Dad and Claire had helped me find a seat and hoisted my bags onto the overhead rack, and we'd finished our good-byes.

"You're not bringing anything?" I asked as Izzy sat down next to me.

"My needs are few. I travel light." He looked around the train and frowned. "I hope this is a good idea, Lucas. I can't remember the last time I was out of the city. Yes, I can. I went to the bureau's annual convention in Pleasant Valley. Big surprise. I didn't like it. What if I don't like it in Connecticut? What if annoyances are nonexistent? What if there's no need for me?" The train had come out of the tunnel now. He looked out the window at the bustling New York streets, the fire escapes, the run-down buildings. "They need me here, Lucas. There's so much for me to do in New York—"

"There's tons to correct in Connecticut, too," I said. I'd already told him he'd feel right at home in the Fairfield bookstore. I'd told him how the annoyance level at Bentley Prep never dipped below a seven. I'd stopped feeling sad about leaving. I was getting excited. We'd passed through the Bronx now, into Westchester. There were fewer big buildings now, more regular houses, and way more trees.

"This train will be making all stops," the conductor called. "First stop . . ."

"Oy!" Izzy said as we pulled into the station. "Why is everything so clean here? This snow is whiter than in the

Himalayas! And why are all these people smiling? From the look of it, this place barely makes it to mildly irksome! Are we in Connecticut yet?" he asked a few stops later. "It might reassure me if we take a reading." He felt in his pocket. "Wait a minute. Where's the irkostat?"

"It's not in your pocket?" I said. "What about the other pocket?"

He stood up and patted all his pockets. "Lucas, you're sure you don't have it?"

"I haven't had it since I gave it back to you," I said. "Yesterday morning. You put it in the laundry bag."

His face went white. "And you didn't see it when you unpacked the wash?"

"I only unpacked mine," I said. "Not Gladys's."

"Oy." He put his head in his hands. "This is a disastrophe! The Correct function in the hands of Madam Kidney? I can see it now: corporate execs dressed in OshKosh B'Gosh, singing 'I'm a Little Teapot'; four-star restaurants serving kidney oatmeal surprise; cops making criminals sit on the bench and take a time-out; life grinding to a halt while everyone waits for everyone else to say the magic word. . . . How could this have happened? What was I thinking? I wasn't thinking!"

"Do we need to go back?" I said. We could get off at the next stop. I could call Mom and tell her I'd be late.

"Back?" He shook his head. "You don't go back, Lucas. You know that by now. You go forward. And you're coming to New York soon for a visit. When did you say that was? Martin Luther King Day?"

I looked at him. "You'll come with me?"

"I was operating on that assumption."

"How is that going to work? In fact"—we'd never discussed where he'd stay or how he'd live—"how is any of this going to work?"

"I can't believe you're asking me that," he said. "With all the things that have worked so far, that you've made work, things you never in your wildest imaginings dreamed could work out . . ."

He was right.

"You know something," I said. "The irkostat will be fine with Gladys. Gladys won't touch it. She can barely use the microwave. She's terrified of the remote. And you yourself said it's a hunk of junk without your mental messages. The only one who might mess around with it is Calvin."

"Hmmm. Two is a touch young for an apprentice," he said. "I'd feel happier if we could disable it, or send it a mental message to ignore them. No, I know! I'll send it a message to tuck itself somewhere safe. We've never tested the range of my mental messages, but my guess is it's long."

"Can I tell you something else?" I said. I'd been thinking about this for a while. "It might even be better that we can't just turn it over to the bureau. I was getting a little worried about letting their engineers make more of them. I mean, they'd be giving irkostats to the same guys who confiscated the kids' snacks, right?"

He was nodding. "The very same."

"So do we really want thousands of irkostats in their hands?"

"I've been worrying about that too," he said.

"And you know what else I'm thinking? The irkostat didn't open the nuts, did it?"

"No," he said. "That was me."

"And it was you who changed everyone's mood in Book World that day, right? And unsticking the kid's jacket from his braces? That wasn't the irkostat either—"

"Oh, we've got plenty of powers," he said. "Powers are not the problem. We've got more powers than we can shake a finger at, some as yet radically underutilized. No, you're right, as usual. Technology is only one small part."

"So, then, we're still in business?"

"Oh, *absolutamente!*" he said.

I wondered where he'd rank my friend Dan on the Gribitz scale, what he'd think of the mall, if he could ride a bike. I wondered if there'd be an e-mail from Alex when I got home. There was a week of vacation left. And then school. School would feel like a whole different thing with Izzy around. It might feel different anyway.

No. Not might. Would.

The train was slowing now. "Fairfield!" the conductor called. "Station stop is Fairfield."

"Izzy, that's us," I said. "We're here!"

Mom was on the platform, holding Aslan on his leash. The train stopped. I jumped up and grabbed my bags from the rack. I could see Aslan's eyes brighten as the train doors opened. His ears went up and his tail started wagging.

"That's my dog!" I told Izzy. "And my mom."

"I knew that, Lucas," he said. "Without the irkostat."

I put my jacket on and zipped it. I wondered if Dan was home.

"Come on, let's go," I told Izzy. "Put your coat on."

He was still sitting there.

"Izzy, aren't you coming?"

Mom had started waving.

He took my hand, then shook his head. "Nah," he said. "It looks great here. Really. Annoying in a good way, good in an annoying way . . . but I've been thinking about this the whole trip. I'm a New York City kind of guy, Lucas."

"What about the bookstore?" I said. "What are you going to do about the bureau? What if you need help with something? What if you need me?"

"Don't you worry about that," he said. "We'll figure it out as we go along."

Mom was waving both arms now. Aslan's tail was wagging so hard it looked like if I didn't get to him soon, it might fall off.

"It's been good, Lucas." Izzy gave my hand a squeeze.

I squeezed his back. "It's been great," I said.

Then I let go of his hand and started for the door. "I've gotta hop."